SCRAP METAL ANGEL

NICOLA KAPRON

DUCK PRINTS PRESS

Schenectady, New York

Scrap Metal Angel
Copyright © 2024 Nicola Kapron

Front cover design by Rascal Hartley

Edited by Nina Waters
Print Manuscript formatting by Hermit Prints
E-book formatting by Nina Waters

Published by Duck Prints Press, LLC
Schenectady, New York
duckprintspress.com

ISBN (ePub Edition): 978-1-962488-19-8
ISBN (PDF Edition): 978-1-962488-18-1
ISBN (Print edition): 978-1-962488-20-4

Tags:
Genre: Fantasy with Technology
Rating: Mature
Trigger Warnings: body horror (graphic descriptions), death of a parent (past), death of a sibling (past), death of a spouse (past), gore (graphic descriptions), misgendering, minor character death, violence (graphic descriptions)
Relationships: friends, siblings, twins
Character Features: bipoc, magic use, murderer, non-human character, secret identity, sentient construct, tattoos, trans man
Other Tags: angst, be gay solve crimes, dimension jumping, magical mishaps, murder, past tense, resurrection, second chances, third person limited (multiple) point of view

CONTENTS

1

EVEN A GATEKEEPER couldn't bring back the dead, but people still blamed them when they failed to. Adrian Somer could feel baleful stares coming from all directions as he walked through the Winfrey Station subway terminal, following the sound of battle. The fabric of this reality was fighting the teeth and claws of creatures that had learned to feed on it. Reality was losing. As a Gatekeeper, it was his job to fix that. He hadn't been able to save the three members of station staff who'd already been killed, but hopefully he could stop the destruction there.

The waiting area was closed down and packed with survivors. Some of them were staff permanently assigned to Platform 7, including a few practitioners. They, at least, had known about what lay underneath the platform. The rest were unfortunate passengers who'd been mid-transit when disaster struck. One of them was a small blond staring silently into the middle distance, and that sight brought memories of another blond boy Adrian couldn't afford to dwell on. Not now, anyway. He shoved thoughts of Leslie down and kept walking. Dazed mumbling and quiet sobs echoed in his ears as clearly as the clash of bone and tooth on wood, concrete, and power.

Three bodies had been lined up in the corner of the room, at once out of the way and impossible to miss. A tarp had been draped haphazardly over them. As he passed, a pair of dead eyes stared accusingly through a gap in the fabric. He looked away and focused on the figure standing by the hastily barricaded stairs. The station's chief on-staff practitioner was an older man with a snow-white beard, a broad frame covered in bloodstains and scrapes, and an air of great discomfort. Adrian couldn't tell whether the discomfort was from the circumstances or Adrian's presence alone.

Hopefully, it was mostly the former. Adrian was already more talkative than most Keepers, and he didn't bother with the so-called uniform of his position, the illusion of an ominous shadowy cloak that concealed Keepers' identities at the cost of being a complete PR disaster. Instead, he was wearing a professional suit and he'd finger-combed his blond hair as neatly as he could while teleporting over. He hadn't slept more than three hours in as many days and he suspected that it showed. He did his best to smile reassuringly as he drew near. There wasn't much else he could do to make himself more approachable.

"What am I dealing with?" he asked as soon as he was within hearing distance.

The old man grimaced, his eyes skittering away from Adrian. His magical signature was a jangle of metallic sounds—triangle, perhaps—mixed with the repetitive pounding of three piano keys. Solid, reliable, and, right now, panicking. "Portal's opened up again. Some fool new kid decided to ignore the briefing and cleaned up the paint."

Oh, for— "Didn't you promise my partner you'd tell the other staff about the seal?"

"I did!" the old man snapped. "Ain't my fault they won't listen to their elders! It's a miracle most of them listened when I realized the seal was failing. 'Who believes in magic these days,' indeed." He scoffed loudly, then flinched when he remembered who Adrian was. Or rather, *what* Adrian was. "A-anyway, don't think we should try repainting the seal on the underworld. Seems like an invitation for this to happen again."

"I agree." Adrian peered at the pile of furniture and cement blocking off the staircase to the underground, listening closely. The makeshift barricade was held together with magic and spite. It had bought the station enough time for him to arrive, but it wouldn't hold much longer. He needed to act fast. "What kind of practitioner are you?"

With a wary glance, the old man rolled up his sleeve. There was a thick golden bracer wrapped around his wrist like a watch, covered with a series of raised bumps and lowered indents that looked something like braille. "Tactile."

Magic was a tricky and highly subjective thing. Each practitioner's experiences with it were different, but they could generally be divided into the five senses: sight, sound, smell, touch, and taste. Each had their strengths and their weaknesses, but a tactile practitioner took valuable time tracing out or carving spells—time that Adrian couldn't afford to waste. "Then stay here. Protect the others if anything escapes. I'll go down alone."

For a moment, the old man hesitated. Then he nodded sharply and stepped aside, still not meeting Adrian's eyes. "Good luck, Keeper Somer."

If luck played a factor in this, Adrian wouldn't have been running around fixing magical disasters since the sun had risen that morning, when he'd been jolted out of fitful sleep by the sound of screaming. First, it had been an amateur practitioner accidentally lighting her entire apartment building on fire. She'd been rather nice to deal with, actually—she hadn't internalized the horror of being caught by a Gatekeeper, so she'd listened seriously to his scolding and then pressed some muffins on him as thanks for saving her home. Then a series of very non-magical trucks had tentacles explode out of their engines because some magical auto mechanics were testing new enchantments on innocent drivers. After that, someone needed to force some confused extra-dimensional squid back into their own realities and erase the memories of every ordinary person involved, or at least bind them to silence. Just as someone was going to have to do here, once the fight was over and the seal repaired, and arrange for the bodies to be cleaned up. It never ended, and there were rarely muffins. Adrian was one of the world's greatest practitioners, plugged directly into the Gates—the source of all magic in the universe—and he was still barely staying on top of things in one city.

When Adrian had first had the power and responsibility of a Keeper thrust on him, his mentor Theresa had spoken dreamily of the days before security cameras, cell phones, and, oh yes, the internet. At the time, his ravaged soul aching and his old name freshly buried, he hadn't understood the appeal. He did now. Keeping magic hidden must've been so much simpler back then. A few quick memory alterations and some rumours spread about ghosts or spirits, and you were done. Unethical, but easy.

He whistled sharply, pouring a spell of movement into the piercing sound. Then he stepped forward and walked through the barrier. The stairway was shallow but dark, the air filled with blood and acidic, alien smells. It had been less than an hour since the seal broke and the portal under Platform 7 tried to swallow the whole building again. The portal that his partner, Kade Mauzy, was supposed to have dealt with months ago. Either she'd slipped up when re-applying the seal after the last break-out or the breach was growing more severe. He hummed a shield spell as he walked, low and steady, wondering how many of the surviving witnesses had taken pictures. And how many of those pictures would come back to bite him.

The second his foot hit the floor, concrete exploded upward and a swarm of things that looked like ferrets crossed with beetles surged up to snap at him with three-jawed mouths. Lovely.

"Please stop," he said, flaring the shield spell outward with the singsong pitch of his voice. "Why do you want to eat us, anyway? Humans taste awful, I assure you."

The only answer was high-pitched insectoid chittering, no recognizable emotions or meanings attached, which was about what he'd expected. The last time the portal had opened, it had almost gotten the whole street, and he'd had to go down and beat the inhabitants of the alternate dimension it connected to into submission. Life would be a lot easier if he could just negotiate with them, or threaten them, or something. Unfortunately, these guys were far enough from human understanding that communication had proved impossible—and unlike the confused extra-dimensional squid, they wouldn't leave willingly. They had to be forced back, and because their armour would protect them from anything up to and including anti-tank rounds, it had to be a practitioner who did it. And because it was a city-owned station, doing so was the Keepers' responsibility. Lord knew none of the corporate mages would protect city property. Hard to bank on civic pride in a hidden society, even one where secrecy was becoming increasingly difficult.

Whenever Adrian could, he tried to walk the line between keeping the hidden world hidden and keeping people safe by making sure ordinary humans in dangerous areas had an idea of what they should watch out for. Sometimes that backfired, because nothing made a certain type of person more determined to break the rules than being told there was magic involved. It would be nice to leave most of these jobs to the city's police or firefighters. Unfortunately, the practitioners working secretly in those organizations couldn't bring the sheer magical might to bear that he could, even at his worst.

Adrian wasn't at his worst now. He'd been sleeping better recently, which meant more strength he could spare to throw his magical weight around. That was important because using magic was exhausting. Every time the creatures threw themselves into his barrier, a little more of that strength drained away. An ordinary practitioner—one without a Keeper's connection to the Gates—would probably have lost consciousness from the strain. He was mostly cold. Even with his coat, it was freezing down here. He continued humming the barrier spell under his breath as he rubbed his hands together in a feeble attempt to warm up.

"Just give up already. If I have to pull another all-nighter because of you—"

Finally, the chitinous horde drew back. Adrian hummed louder and extended his barrier, pushing them farther. They screeched and swiped at the shimmering air as he herded them back down into the dusty, chewed-up crawlspace under the platform. This place was supposed to be a maintenance tunnel. Now it looked like Hell's car park and smelled like it, too. Adrian kept the barrier up until every single ferrety bastard had hopped down into the circle of raw, reddened flesh that grew smoothly from dead concrete. Once he was sure they were gone, he sang the barrier solid, hooked it into the remains of the last barrier Kade had set up around the portal, and finally stopped casting. Then he sat down heavily and breathed for just long enough for his hands to stop shaking.

After a minute, he pried himself off the pavement and started heading back. Time to hand clean-up over to the old man in the station crew, who'd plaster over the hole with illusions and the sudden impulse to go literally anywhere else. Adrian fully expected a new disaster to hit before that was over. Even if by some miracle it didn't, he was overdue to check in with his partner. It had been about two weeks since he'd seen Kade. They'd made plans to meet and share notes at 10 p.m., and it was almost midnight now. If he didn't bring a new emergency to the meet-up, she would.

The hidden world's strongest magical practitioners—at least, the strongest practitioners who could still be called human—should be able to stop things like this from happening. But sometimes, all they could do was bandage up the wounds and clean the blood off the floor.

Adrian cast one last glance at the sealed portal and wrinkled his nose. "This job would be so much easier if people would just listen."

The creatures living under the platform screamed. Their voices were muffled by the seal, but the power in the sound scraped against his ears like a blade to the soul. He turned his back on them and climbed the stairs above the platform. Each step restored a bit of his energy, fresh power oozing up from his connection to the Gate. By the time he reached the barricade and phased back through, he felt almost human again. The old man looked happy to see him. In a surprising turn of events, so did the rest of the survivors.

There was still a numbness to the crowd as he stepped into the warm electric light. More than a few of the people here were in shock; he advised the station staff to call emergency services before sending anyone home. Then he had to gently fight his way through a grateful mob that had never heard of Gatekeepers and only knew he'd saved their lives.

Honestly, the thanks were more intimidating than the creatures living under the platform.

A kid smiled at him as he extracted himself. "Thanks, mister."

For a moment, Adrian saw another blond boy smiling at him, narrow-eyed and brimming with mischief. Then he blinked and the illusion was gone. Leslie always had been terribly respectful to strangers until they realized what a little monster he was. Especially if they managed to impress him, or worse, had something he wanted. Adrian had spent so much of his life chasing Leslie into trouble that, eight years after Leslie had died, he still saw his twin everywhere he looked.

Even a Keeper couldn't bring back the dead, no matter how much he wished otherwise.

"Stay out of trouble," Adrian murmured, and saw himself out.

KADE WAS ALREADY in the diner when he arrived, her presence marked by a soft, phantom chorus of woodwinds mixed with the harsh squeal of an electric guitar. Jarring, distinctive, magical, human—the signature of her existence in this reality. It was so strong it almost blocked out the soft chime that signaled a practitioners-only establishment and the equally soft hum of a Keeper's professional illusion. She usually wore the illusion when meeting with him in public, despite the inevitable effect it had on every other practitioner around them. The whole building was locked in a terrified silence that only grew worse as he stepped inside. The girl behind the front desk gave him a wild-eyed look, the soft harpsichord of her magical signature stuttering, and bared her teeth in what was supposed to be a smile.

"Welcome, Keeper Somer! Do you have a table?"

He nodded.

Her knuckles were white around her clipboard. "Excellent! Right this way."

The waitress led him to a corner booth near the window, her hands shaking even worse than his. Adrian didn't point that out. He was no stranger to being feared. Besides, he was too busy searching for his partner. The faint sound of her professional illusion drew his eyes to the bench she was slouched on; the façade was designed not to affect Keepers, so he could see behind the ominous shadow. What lay underneath was, to put it bluntly, a mess. She had one brown cheek pressed against the table, fine white hair pooling around her. Her latex-and-tulle party dress was stained with sweat and spilled alcohol. She was absently drawing a butterfly on the cheek facing up with a sharpie. As he watched, the remnants of a black eye faded away. She didn't look up when he slid in beside her, but then, she didn't need to.

"Hey, stranger." Her voice was rusty from use. Headache, he judged, combined with sleep deprivation and possibly a light concussion. Nothing too serious. "You're late."

The waitress retreated without asking for their order. Adrian let her go without comment. "Something came up. Rough night?"

"Isn't it always?" Kade tilted her head until he could see both her dark eyes. "Guess who shut down some wannabe supervillain leading a magical coup? This girl."

"What, seriously? You should've called me." The Keepers' duty was twofold: first, to protect the Gates, the single greatest source of raw power in existence and the fulcrum on which reality rested, from tampering by anyone or anything; and second, to protect those whose lives were affected by magic. A magic-driven coup would affect a lot of people. "What were they couping against?"

"Us, obviously, but first they went after our puppets in the city council. Because we have those."

Adrian blinked slowly. "We have puppets?"

"Don'tcha know? All politicians are secretly in the Keepers' pockets. So a group of well-intentioned rebels gotta hack our records, steal control of the Gates, and use them to overthrow the whole corrupt system." She scoffed. "I'd be first on the bandwagon, if, y'know, we actually controlled anything."

He considered that for a moment. "If we were secretly in charge of everything, I think we'd be able to delegate more."

"Now I wish we were secretly in charge of everything. Hey, did they bring my order yet?"

Adrian shook his head. "Waitress left."

"Figures."

He followed her stare to the window. Outside, downtown was bright and busy. Inside, their reflections on the glass revealed how everyone else in the restaurant was seeing the two of them. He looked the same as always: a slim blond man with hair too long to look professional—right now, it was chin-length, thank God; any longer and the heart-deep ache of dysphoria would start kicking in on top of everything else—and deep circles under his eyes. She showed up as an anonymous, hooded shape wreathed in pitch-black shadow. Within the hidden world, that illusion was as iconic as it was terrifying. Even outside the hidden world, there was a reason hooded shadows were associated with death and disaster: it was a Keeper's job to stop magic from blowing up in everyone's faces, whether that meant cleaning up after someone else's mistakes or protecting the Gates from anyone stupid enough to open them.

Well, the Second Gate and any more that might lie beyond, anyway. The First Gate was already open. It had been open since before recorded history. No one knew what had been on the other side because no one could remember what life was like before the defences around it failed.

"You need to stop going out in public in uniform," he said. "You scared the waitress out of her wits."

"Give me a break, I came straight here from the coup-thwarting."

"You got here before me."

"I'm too tired to set up a new illusion and I don't want my civilian identity tied up with you, Mr. Publicly-A-Keeper. Some of us still want to live a normal life sometimes."

Adrian tried to imagine living normally, or even pretending to, and failed. He'd been a Keeper since he was seventeen years old, recruited right out of a magical ritual that had failed so badly it had killed his brother and their guardian and almost destroyed him as well. At his lowest point, he'd stumbled into the street and the fabric of reality had swallowed him and spit him out. When he'd opened his eyes, he'd been standing in front of the Second Gate, and a terrible power had forced itself into him. It had been the second worst experience of his life, beaten only by what had come just before it.

Leslie's dead face flashed through Adrian's mind—frozen smile, surprised blue eyes, red hole in the center of his forehead. He'd been so quiet lying there. In seventeen years, Leslie had never been that quiet before. In a way, that silence had been the worst part.

"It's so stupid that people are scared of us," Kade grumbled. "We're not hiding any more than any other practitioners. We have a website with our mission statement on it, for crying out loud."

"They didn't read the mission statement."

She groaned and settled her forehead against the tabletop again. "How about we make it illegal to not read the mission statement? How about we do that?"

"That's unethical."

"Not very. Better than leading a coup, anyway." She yawned hugely. "I'm too tired for this."

"Then let's speed this meeting up so we can go home and nap."
It was a good idea for both of them. Magic could do a lot of things,
but it couldn't replace sleep any more than it could bring back the
dead—not fully, anyway. Thoughts would still slow. Reflexes would
still dull. If Kade wasn't up for a full meeting, she probably wasn't up
for spellcasting any longer. Adrian was more rested than Kade, but
he'd still been working all day. And they couldn't afford to succumb
to exhaustion with the whole magical community circling them like
sharks.

It all came down to the Gates in the end. Nobody wanted to hear
there was an enormous reservoir of power and they couldn't touch
it. Never mind that touching it wasn't safe for anyone. Even now,
Adrian could feel the channels carved into his soul burning. They
hurt when he used too much magic and when he used too little.
They ensured he'd never kill himself by running out of magic and
chained him to a duty he hadn't asked for. Above all else, they promised power. The kind of power that destroyed you. Seven out of ten
Keeper candidates tried to open the Gates when the universe offered
them the chance and died after triggering the defences layered around
the Gates—the ones meant to stop anyone from opening them and
ending the world as they knew it. The three who didn't fall for that
temptation spent the rest of their lives trying to stop anyone from
being faced with that terrible opportunity. The ominous uniform
was the most glamorous part of the whole thing.

But wasn't it more fun to imagine Keepers as some kind of secret
police? That was so much more interesting than a bunch of overtired
workers running around wearing spooky illusions, wielding power
siphoned from a dam barred from public access for safety reasons.
That way, people could feel justified when they made plans to sneak
through the barricades, blow the dam wide open, and flood the
planet.

"I wanna eat first," Kade mumbled. "Or drink a smoothie, anyway.
Where's our waiter?"

Adrian hummed a quick listening spell, three notes ascending in pitch, and grimaced. "Hyperventilating in the bathroom."

"Damn. We got time to wait?"

He shrugged. "Nothing's hanging over my head."

"Me either. I'll give her…" Kade rolled her head to the other side and glanced at the wall clock. "Five minutes to come out before I go after her. That should be enough time, right?"

"Probably." Adrian wondered if he should volunteer to find the waitress instead. She might react slightly better to a Keeper who had a face knocking politely outside her hiding place than a faceless Keeper materializing inside it. "You should eat more."

"If I eat more, I'll throw up. 'Sides, I gotta eat breakfast like five times with five different guys tomorrow, none of whom know each other. Such is the price of information gathering."

"Spying, more like."

She arched an eyebrow. "Got a problem with that?"

Adrian said nothing and continued staring out the window. It wasn't that he was particularly against her keeping tabs on what the Corporate, NGO, and Independent practitioners in their territory were up to; her decision to turn her civilian identity into an information sponge just put a bad taste in his mouth. The idea of bending people to your will with a false, smiling face made him feel cold. But then, so did the decision to keep a civilian identity at all. He'd changed his name to lay his past self to rest alongside his brother. The person he'd been back then was dead and buried along with the life he'd planned, one carefully chosen by two kids who shared everything, including the certainty that they were both boys no matter what anyone told them.

Everything he had left, he poured into his duty. It was easier to fill the hole Leslie had left that way.

"Don't scare the waitress too badly."

"I won't, you softie." Kade yawned again. "God, I'm tired. Nothing else better happen tonight."

The second the words were out of her mouth, the whole city screamed.

Adrian sat bolt upright, the harsh G minor notes of a barrier spell leaping from his tongue. A shield of pale blue light crackled to life around the diner just in time. He heard the sudden failure of its wards echo in his bones—a silence so thick he could choke on it. An overflowing of power, and then an utter absence. It felt like losing someone precious again.

"Oh, what the hell!" Kade spilled out onto her feet as thick black lines wrote themselves to life over her dark skin, tattoos flaring to life. Her eyes went blank, then zeroed in on something he couldn't see. "Crap. Adrian, the seals are failing."

"Which ones?" he said tightly, the repeating notes of the barrier spell still playing in his head. The main impact had passed, but whatever was out there, it had hit hard. "Runes? Wards? Protections?"

"All of them."

That didn't make any sense. If every single point of stored or anchored magic in the city failed, then the results would be—

From the vacuum rose more discordant notes than he could count: failed spells, small holes in reality, and much, much worse. With a metallic screech, the building across the street began crumpling in on itself. Not collapsing—imploding. People fought to drag themselves outside as the splintered upper floors caught fire. The gravitational anomaly stayed limited to that building. The fire spread. A massive sinkhole opened in the street with the sound of grinding teeth. The closest cars careened into the hole just as a set of enormous, lamprey-like jaws closed overtop. In the distance, sirens began to wail.

Adrian shot to his feet as well. "We need to get out there."

Kade was already halfway to the door. The second she got outside, she slammed her fist into the sidewalk. Black ink slithered down her skin and hooked into the concrete, and from there, the buildings. Everywhere her tattoos touched, the ground stopped shaking. "I'll hold things together. Evacuate people, now!"

He slammed as much power into the barrier around the restaurant as he could, creating a bubble of safety. Then he ran into the flames. Figures stumbled toward him, choking. Teenagers with singed hair and smeared make-up. Seniors fighting with canes and walkers. Parents carrying their children. He put the fire out first, then reached into the major chords and sang the scorched flooring into a gentle slope. Heads lifted as he passed, looking at him with something between fear and hope. "Head to the restaurant across the street," he called, voice buzzing with a tone that would blur their memories later. "It's safe there."

"How do you know that?" a mother asked shrilly, a coughing child cradled in her arms.

"I made sure of it," he said grimly.

Some of the crowd moved as directed, but she dug her heels in. "What happened? What did you do?" Her voice went sharp. "Who are you? You're not a cop! Are you with them?"

She didn't specify who "them" was meant to refer to. The anger and suspicion alone drew attention from their surroundings, but Adrian didn't have time to answer questions or soothe people right now. He pushed through the crowd, jaw clenched so tightly it ached. People were still fleeing the collapsing buildings. The lamprey-sinkhole opened again, the remains of its meal nowhere to be seen. An explosion went off a few blocks away. Bright flames licked up into the sky.

Adrian ran toward the light. He was the only one who did.

II

SHION MATREVA PACED through the interior of the warehouse, hand raised to shield her eyes from the glare, and checked her watch. Fifteen minutes to midnight. Every corner was brightly illuminated. The ritual was not going to fail because of an unfortunately placed shadow. Most of the concrete floor was taken up by an intricate diagram, layer upon layer of carvings, paints, and raised textures forming a single massive spell. It was the kind of large-scale spell an auditory practitioner like her would only be able to build in concert with hundreds, if not thousands, of other spellcasters. The tactile and visual practitioners she'd sought out had been able to build off her theory and make the ritual reality with only thirteen people. Every sense and every style of magic, intertwined and incorporated into a single, beautiful whole. And visuals and textures could be so much more permanent than sound, scent, or taste. Less efficient, perhaps, but excellent for building up power for grand spells like this.

Just listening to the diagram sing around her hammered in the enormity of what she'd done. It had taken eight years to reach this point. Eight years since her beloved Yves had been stolen from her. Eight years since she'd embarked on this desperate, brilliant plan to get him back.

All around her, the coven was adding the finishing touches to the diagram that would bring them to the Second Gate—the huge cosmic structure that stood between life and death. Small, lively Tina was tapping away last-minute details with a chisel in uncharacteristic silence. Tall, thin Soo-bin was standing behind Charlie's huge form, watching over his shoulder with glowing eyes as he laboriously painted the details. Shion stood off to the side, surveying everyone's work and conserving her strength. If her calculations were correct, the ritual would require almost all of it.

But it would be worth it to have Yves in her arms again.

Janine, a plump young woman with a hand-knitted sweater and dyed black hair, stood up and stretched. "Third quadrant's ready, Ms. Matreva."

Shion's heart leaped. It was so hard to restrain herself, but she gave Janine a warm smile and headed over at a carefully unhurried pace. "We're collaborating on a project that will change everything, Janine. Please, call me Shion."

"Doesn't feel right. You were my teacher before we got into all of this." Janine waved at the bustle around them.

Shion followed the gesture with her eyes, listening. Everything sounded like it was in its proper place. The whorls of colour and texture would mean more to someone who interpreted magic through sight or touch, but to Shion, they sang sweetly. A door waiting to be opened. A hand waiting to be pulled to safety.

They should work. It should all work.

"It looks good. Thank you, Janine."

Janine shot Shion a quick smile back. She looked so young. Innocent, even. Not at all like a cheerful hacker who'd wheedled important personal information out of countless other practitioners to help set this up. That ability to make herself seem enthusiastic and harmless was why Shion had made Janine her second-in-command, even though Janine was also an auditory practitioner who could barely interact with the ritual's physical components. "How are the safeguards?"

"Fully charged," Shion assured her.

"Any danger of overloading?"

"Not for another day, at least. After that, it'll be a bit touch and go." Shion's smile sharpened, then she got herself under control again. "But if we do this right, it won't matter."

Janine's grin widened. "We're really doing this, aren't we? After all these years, it's hard to believe. I'm really gonna see Mom again."

Yes. Janine's mother, Charlie's daughter, Tina's sister, Maria's father—and, most importantly, Yves—would return to life soon. Happiness was close enough to touch. On impulse, Shion reached out and gave Janine's hand a firm squeeze. "You're not dreaming. In a few more minutes, we'll see them all again."

"Assuming the Keepers don't break down the door and murder us." Her voice was light and playful, but there was a layer of fear underneath.

Shion gave her hand another squeeze before letting go. "Don't worry about it," she said, turning back to the diagram. "When I updated the ritual, I took care to avoid anything that would broadcast our location. The Keepers can't sense what we're doing. They aren't even aware we exist."

The old version of her creation was certainly stored in the archives of the Gatekeepers, but any alerts they had attached to tell them if the design was being used were linked to power output. Shion had been very careful to keep the drain this version exerted on its surroundings subtle. Then she'd layered it behind so many protective wards that even she couldn't sense it from outside this building. There was a limit to how much power a practitioner could draw upon without breaking the fragile legal code of their secret world. Anyone who violated that agreement and got caught would immediately have the Gatekeepers descend on them. She'd broken that limit four times over. Raw power chimed beneath her feet—enough to sink the coast, repel an artillery strike, or save a life.

Mathematically speaking, bringing back the dead was not difficult. And Shion had had eight years to nail down the practical application. This would work. She had to wonder why nobody else had tried it before.

Janine sighed, stepping up beside her. "I know. I just—I've seen them in action. They're like horror-movie monsters. If they find us, they'll squash us like bugs, and no one will be able to do anything about it. That much power…"

Shion closed her eyes. For a moment, she was twenty-six again, sitting in a cell, clutching what was left of her proposal with shaking hands. She'd made the mistake of going to the Keepers for help, assuming the hidden world's shadowy watchdogs had enough of a conscience to understand how much she needed the man she loved back. Instead, they'd blacklisted her name, put her on a watchlist, and locked her up in some kind of house arrest for daring to speak about letting non-Keepers use the Gates. She couldn't get out because the woman charged with watching over her could throw around more magic with a single gesture than Shion had used in her whole life.

One year into her captivity, her jailer had been called away for something bigger and more pressing. That was the only reason they'd let her go. Her first year of freedom had been spent constantly checking over her shoulder, waiting for a black-robed figure to step out of the ether and take her back into custody. It hadn't happened yet. The immortal, faceless guardians of magic might have access to power beyond mortal ken, but as a group, they had the same flaws as any organization.

There would be no second chance. Not for her. But if she succeeded, none of that would matter.

"Don't worry about it," Shion repeated, plastering on her most reassuring smile. The constant assurances were irritating, but this close to her goal, she could afford to be magnanimous. "It would take a catastrophe to draw their attention."

Janine's reply sounded suspiciously like "famous last words," but a call of "First quadrant done!" allowed Shion to gracefully ignore it.

The only flaw she found was a smudge of chalk outside the spray-painted lines. Easily remedied. When she stood up, Charlie and

Soo-bin waved her toward the second quadrant, their sunken eyes bright with hope.

"How does it look?" Charlie rumbled. He was a big man, broad and thick as a tree trunk, possessed of a fierce vitality. He'd lost his daughter, and he'd been well on his way to drinking himself to death when Shion had found him.

Soo-bin, a rail-thin woman with long hair and spectacles, peered over his shoulder with piercing eyes. Her stare was razor sharp. Shion met it without flinching. After all, she had nothing to hide.

"It looks good so far. Let me give it a closer examination." Shion knelt down to listen properly. A single sour note would spoil the whole spell.

After a moment, Soo-bin knelt to join her. "Charlie and I double-checked each other's work. There shouldn't be anything out of place."

The words were sharp, but Soo-bin spoke with breathless anticipation. Soo-bin had lost her son; she hadn't been self-destructing quite as badly as Charlie had when Shion approached her, but she'd still leaped at the chance to have her child back. As any good parent should. The two of them had bonded over their shared losses, though Charlie had also latched onto little Maria as something of a replacement daughter. Shion regretted that she hadn't been able to find a powerful, grieving boy to recruit; giving Soo-bin a surrogate child to mother would have bound their little coven even tighter.

Her examination turned up no flaws in the paint or chalk. The second quadrant was perfect, and she made sure to tell them so, impressing that she couldn't have set up this ritual without their hard work. Holding a group together was never easy, especially one as ragtag as this. Everyone had to know they were doing their part and being valued for it or the whole coven would splinter.

The fourth quadrant, finished by the youngest of the coven, fourteen-year-old Maria, had a sour note in the mix. One of the spray-painted glyphs was misshapen. Shion sank to one knee and traced the orange curve, frowning slightly. "Were you rushing here,

Maria?"

The girl took a second look and wilted. "I'm sorry. I didn't notice."

"It's fine," Shion assured her. The spiral was on the diagram's outermost layer; there was no need to shuttle excess magic out of the way before editing it. She reached out to trace the glyph again, humming. The paint peeled off the floor under her fingers, accompanied by a sound like the distant chime of bells.

"H-how…?"

Shion smiled at Maria's dumbstruck expression. "This is what magic is all about—erasing your mistakes. Why don't you try painting that again?"

Maria nodded and scurried back over to the spray can, a silver anklet marked with raised carvings and bells jingling as she moved. Despite the sound, she was a tactile practitioner. She would only be able to cast a few spells using the sensations the anklet caused, but that was fine. Shion had helped Maria pick out the perfect ones to help protect the ritual when she'd recruited the girl. Any other spells would be unnecessary. Shion already had all the ones she needed from Maria. Edits done, Shion stood up, stretched, and made her way back to the centre of the circle. Maria should be able to fix the diagram without Shion hovering over her shoulder.

Sure enough, she caught the sound of tiny chains and running footsteps a minute later. "Finished!"

This time, there wasn't a single spot of paint out of place. Shion grinned and ruffled Maria's dark hair. "Well done."

Maria beamed before schooling her features into seriousness. "Are we ready to start now?"

Shion took one last look around the room. "Yes. All right, everyone, please get into position!"

The twelve other members of her coven stopped milling around and made their way to the edges of the diagram, spacing themselves evenly around its perimeter. This was the only part of the ritual they'd been able to rehearse, and it had gone off without a hitch.

Her stomach clenched. She could only hope the rest would go as smoothly.

With a raise of her hand, the rumble of chanting and rhythmic stamps began. It wove into the hum, rising and falling around that steady pillar of sound. Shion waited until the song had reached a fever pitch before joining in, casting a thread of power into the diagram. It drank her magic up greedily. The lines of chalk, spray paint, and carved designs began to glow. The hum rose in volume until it thundered in her ears, incredible concentrations of power roaring overhead.

One final invocation, and the air above the diagram tore open. The void yawned before her, absolute darkness pierced with a single point of light. There was power here, but not the kind a human could easily use.

The coven fell silent. The sound of their breathing was drowned out by the roar around them.

Shion steeled herself and stepped forward, reaching into the portal. A bright pulse went through the diagram as the distance—and the multitude of Keeper-made wards—between her hand and her objective disappeared. The light coalesced into a structure of stark whites and dead greys. Bone and pitted metal spikes coiled together, held in place by crusted black soil and shadow. Cold rolled over her, bringing with it the scent of raw metal and grave dirt. The sheer presence of it took her breath away.

She'd poured over every scrap of information on the Gates available to the public and more than a few that weren't. Everything led to this, the Second Gate, the one that was still closed. This was the pillar that upheld the world as she knew it. Behind it lay nothing short of death itself. To open it was to irrevocably change the world, but all she needed to do was crack it.

A moment later, she found what she was looking for: a specific bone in the centre. She didn't recognize the creature whose skeleton it had once belonged to, assuming it had ever been alive, but that didn't matter. About two-thirds of the way up, there was a crack. A flaw. An opening.

Shion. Shion. Shion.

Soft whispers echoed in her ears, piercing through the hum. They put her at ease. Yves was behind the Gate, waiting for her. All she had to do was open the way.

Her fingers brushed the surface of the Second Gate.

And everything went wrong.

It happened in slow motion. Instead of moving, the bone snapped down the middle. Shion caught a glimpse of sickly marrow before a metallic blur dragged itself through the opening and flew at her. There was no time to dodge.

The Gate was still whispering her name.

Shion. Shion.

"Shion!"

The thunder of power cut off. Before her eyes, the portal began to fray. The blur's trajectory twisted; it vanished inches from her face with a noise like a cross between a gunshot and a sob. Shion screamed as the Gate faded back into the darkness, reaching helplessly after it. Hands seized her shoulders and pulled her back. She fought until the portal unravelled entirely and collapsed into a boneless heap as light and void winked out.

Worried voices filled the air as the coven gathered around her. She let the words flow over her like water.

The ritual had failed.

She had failed.

Someone nudged her shoulder insistently. After ignoring it for several seconds, she gave in and looked up. Charlie's harsh features stared down at her. "Shion, what happened?"

It took her a couple of tries to speak without croaking. "Something went wrong. I think—I think something came through, but I don't know what."

"Where is it now?" Maria's voice piped up.

"Somewhere else." The roar had disappeared, but the diagram was still singing—faintly but audibly. With effort, Shion steadied herself. What had gone wrong to end the ritual at such a moment? She reached out for the familiar tune that marked Janine's presence and found it absent. "Janine?"

There was no answer. She glanced at where her second had been standing and froze. Janine lay crumpled on the floor, eyes wide open and head twisted at an impossible angle. A small portion of the chalk diagram—about the size of a human foot—had been erased. Janine's toe was less than an inch away from the smudge's edge.

Janine had called Shion's name when that thing came through. Janine had broken the ritual to keep it away from her. And now, Janine was dead. Hot blood dripped from her mouth and eyes, tell-tale signs of lethal magical backlash. Shion buried the anger before it could do more than blur the edges of her vision and stumbled over to the body. She cupped Janine's cheeks, peering into brown eyes.

It was no use. There was no sound left in Janine, just the absence of a heartbeat and the quiet crunch of rot setting in. Shion bowed her head, pressing her forehead to the corpse's. Janine must have panicked upon seeing the silvery blur approaching and broken the ritual in a hasty attempt to protect Shion. Now she was gone. She had given up everything to preserve their dream and joined Yves beyond the Gate.

"Shion, what do we do?" Maria asked shrilly.

It was difficult for Shion to speak around the lump in her throat. "We clean up. We go over the theory. We try again. Janine died to save us from something that would have seen our cause fail. We can thank her for her sacrifice when we next see her."

This had to be a one-off occurrence. None of her research had implied that things could come through the Gates of their own accord—that information, the Keepers must have hidden. Shion would not allow that mistake to repeat itself. Already she could hear the room relaxing, fearful murmurs smoothing out into whispered assurances. Maria's anklet jangled as she darted onto the diagram, disposable camera in hand. The snap of the shutter broke through the last of Shion's daze. With one final squeeze of Janine's hand, she stood up, wincing as new aches made themselves known. All around her, the coven began following Maria's lead, taking out cameras and measuring instruments. The hum of machinery, augmented and non-augmented, blended smoothly with the soft buzz in Shion's ears.

"Thank you, Janine," she said, the tightness in her throat easing. "I don't know if you can hear me. But I'll tell you again when we open the Gate. This isn't goodbye. It's just a quick parting. I'll see you again soon."

III

THE CITY WAS still standing by sunrise, but it had been a close call. Adrian had pieced this much together from stammering witnesses and his own observations: at midnight on the dot, something big had happened, and in its wake, all the stored magic in the city had been sucked out of its constraints. Every stationary, permanent spell in fifteen kilometres—the ones that were meant to last—had failed simultaneously, including the one Adrian had just fixed. The Corporates and the NGOS were covering their own backs, which left Adrian and Kade to run damage control for everyone else. As the only Keepers in town, they were technically in charge of the official response to the disaster. Unfortunately, the hidden world was prone to factionalism at the best of times. The only reason anyone listened to them was the sheer power two Keepers could bring to bear.

Now that power was going into triage and a series of slapdash spells that were holding most of the city together. The portal under Platform 7 at Winfrey Station had expanded again, swallowing three of the neighbouring platforms, but the chittering swarm had decided to stay put this time. A grocery store had to be hastily evacuated under the excuse of a gas leak when the seal on a dimensional portal stopped working, flooding the store with an inhospitable alien atmosphere. A formerly frozen explosion ripped through an office building, killing three and wounding fifteen more—it was being passed off as a terrorist attack. That living sinkhole had travelled around for a while before opening under an intersection, eating more vehicles, and forcing traffic to a crawl; road safety was going to have fun with what remained of that.

Those were just the tip of iceberg. There was so much more to be dealt with and covered up.

What spell had backfired badly enough to cause this?

If there were more Keepers in the area—

If there were more Keepers, *period*—

But only a dozen or so Keepers were called every year, fewer survived their first contact with the Gates, and training took too long. Adrian had a limited number of coworkers to call on, and that number was "not enough." It was an ugly truth that made itself known in the scratches on his hands, the blood in his shoes, the full-body ache worming its way into his muscles despite the power thrumming through his veins, the mask of blank resignation that had settled over his face after the third time he'd turned a corner to find a crowd of shell-shocked survivors clustered around the hollow shell of a once-crowded apartment building.

Now that the dust had settled, a new problem was set to rear its ugly head. Most practitioners habitually used spells to augment their devices for convenience and to save money. Sometimes that meant magic wands and enchanted vehicles, sometimes it meant phones and computers that never needed charging and never ran out of data—either way, they were using anchored spells. Adrian's gear, including his heavily modded phone, was dead and unresponsive. He'd seen a lot of scared practitioners he'd be happy to delegate things to trying and failing to reactivate machines that smelled of burnt wires. To make matters worse, plenty of practitioners worked in infrastructure. What happened to a city when a sizeable chunk of the tech it was built on stopped working? Thinking about it made his head pound. But then, so did doing everything.

Adrian had been awake and casting for too long. The fraying tune of his magical signature came in faint and distorted to his ears.

His feet ached; they'd definitely started bleeding at some point. The endless stream of raw magic flowing to him from the Gates was all that kept him upright. Kade had taken a break a few hours ago for an emergency nap. She was up again now, slipping on illusion after illusion, gathering information like a professional spy, and keeping people from panicking. That meant it was Adrian's turn to recharge before he started making mistakes.

On any other day, he could just tear a hole in space leading straight to his address, but the fabric of reality was still buzzing like too-tight guitar strings. Walking would be safer for him and everything around him. He'd deliberately picked a quiet path home. It was close to the industrial district, rusting and largely uninhabited, which was sometimes the equivalent of a blinking neon sign reading "SOMETHING IS WRONG." When he first moved here, he'd made a point of dropping by every few days.

Nothing ever happened. Eventually, he'd stopped.

Kade had done the same when she showed up three years ago.

If they ever got a third Keeper assigned to the city, the new kid would probably start the whole song and dance over again.

Adrian had taken this path because it wrapped around to his apartment block and the chances of meeting anyone were low. The accidents—*ha*—had all but emptied the roads. Every once in a while, he'd spot someone walking or driving past, but for the most part, Adrian was alone as he made his way through the darkened streets. Even the stars dimmed and turned their eyes away. He didn't blame them.

As the city's senior Keeper, he still had to check up on the Gates in person, but reality was stretched tight right now. If he were well-rested, the extra tension in space-time wouldn't matter. As it was, he'd probably end up destroying something important—possibly himself—if he didn't get some sleep first.

A distant noise rose above his footsteps. It started small: an electronic buzzing interspersed with clicks, soft and distant and just barely musical. No one was out busking on a night like this, but the sound was too clear to be coming from inside a house. A spell, then. Adrian stopped walking and listened. Where was it coming from?

Once he had a rough idea, he started moving again, listening for any changes in the rhythm. The song grew louder as he closed in, which meant it had a definite source. That could be good; it was much easier to deal with a problem when he had something solid to focus on. It could also be terrible in ways he wasn't up to imagining at the moment. Either way, it wasn't supposed to be here, and he wasn't willing to leave it alone.

As the sound cleared, he realized that what he'd taken for buzzing was actually static. It took a lot to disrupt magic to the point of distortion. The song grew louder and louder, wrapping itself around his thoughts until it was difficult to tell where one ended and the other began. Then, just as suddenly, it began to fade.

Adrian stopped and took a step back. No change. It wasn't a matter of distance, the source itself was fading.

Run-down buildings blurred together. The song was being swallowed by static. The clicks were coming through sharper. More desperate. Was he picking up some kind of distress call? Was something that had withstood the disaster until now about to run out of energy? He racked his brain, but he had no idea what could be making that noise. Please, whatever it was, let it not be about to take the city with it.

He made a sharp turn, following the signal. It was close enough that he could hear soft trills between the clicks, dipping in and out of the static. Like whalesong, but more regular. Trill, click click, burst of static, long trill, static again. Sometimes the trill stretched out, wavering on a high note, and sometimes it sank into static right away, but there was a definite pattern. Woven into that pattern was a feeling of urgency and need.

He reached the mouth of the alley just as a long trill ended and the song subsided into static again.

At first glance, the side street looked empty, but the noise swelled as he approached. This was the place. It was that irritating time of year when the city hadn't quite caught up with nature and the streetlights were still dark. Straining his eyes, he could barely make out crumpled garbage bags and the vague shape of a dumpster. The scent of motor oil cancelled out the reek of its contents; he wasn't sure whether to be thankful. There was a flashlight in one of his bags, but it had been augmented and was now useless. Unless he needed a blunt weapon. Urgency and desperation didn't mean the source of the song was friendly. He reached into his satchel and felt around for the smooth cylinder, still peering into the gloom. The trill had started again, but it was weak. Faltering.

To hell with this.

Adrian wrenched his hand out, flashlight held tightly, and took a step into the alley. The trilling stopped immediately. The next sound that came out of the darkness was all too physical—the scrape of metal against concrete—as something thin and sharp was dragged toward him. He stood his ground, flashlight ready, and waited.

The scraping continued as a shape slowly detached from the rest of the shadows.

With a faint buzz, the streetlights finally flickered on. The outline of a body halted and produced a stream of confused, slightly hysterical clicks.

Adrian remained where he was, squinting to block the worst of the glare. A few soft notes, and the bright spots faded from his vision.

A tangled mess of flesh and metal lay in front of the dumpster, clicking pitifully. A pair of pale arms stretched out in front of something that resembled a human corpse. They had hands but no fingers. Instead, silvery claws dug into the concrete, sending droplets of oil flying when they twitched. The hind limbs were a mess of mangled wires and shredded meat. Adrian's eyes lingered on a tail constructed of sharp-looking blades, a second, leaking stump attached to the base, before landing on the creature's back. The whole surface had been flayed and something torn out. Oil flowed like a fountain, layer upon layer of metal glimmering underneath. They moved like muscle, bunching up and relaxing as the creature began to lift its head. The horrific gashes along either side of its spine didn't stop it.

Then the entity looked at him, oil-slick black hair clinging to a frighteningly familiar face.

Adrian's heart stopped. For a second, he was looking at Leslie, stripped of colour: pale as death, eyes like a shark, black blood slick underneath him as he coiled to spring. If it really were Leslie, then Adrian would deserve whatever his brother's ghost did to him. But the creature didn't pounce. It remained on the ground, limp and bleeding, watching him. With effort, he pushed the comparison out of his head. Whoever this was, it was hurt, maybe dying, and its black eyes pleaded for help. He shoved the flashlight back into his bag and took a tentative step forward.

"If you attack me, we are going to have a problem."

It trilled in response, a tightly woven net of concepts tangled up in the sound. *Confusion-pain-hope?*

The noise wasn't words, it was raw meaning made impossibly dense. He steadied himself before he knelt beside the creature. "I don't know what I can do for you, but I'll try."

Pain.

"I know. Hold on."

The creature proved to be more metal than flesh: a thin veil of torn white skin over black rubber and silver metal. Not what he'd studied during first-aid training, but it bore some resemblance to human anatomy. If they were lucky, he might be able to help.

The entity trilled again, impatience edging into metallic tones.

"I know," Adrian repeated, and opened his bag.

Things went better than they had any right to. The flexible tubes that served as veins and arteries could clamp shut at the ends. Most of them did so on their own. The rest responded well to the tube plugs in Adrian's satchel. Once the leaks had been contained, the creature pushed itself up on its elbows and squinted at him. *Immobility. Request?*

Its legs had been snapped off around mid-thigh, leaving ragged stumps full of wires, gears, and a protruding metal "bone." A medical practitioner or even a skilled mechanic might have been able to figure out a way to dull the pain the creature was clearly feeling. Unfortunately, Adrian was neither. The best thing he could do was wrap a few layers of duct tape around the stumps to protect its insides. That got him some more hissing, but there were no solid alternatives. He did what he could for the twin gashes on its back, but he was operating on an alien species and half his equipment wasn't working, so he defaulted to duct tape there, too.

The creature went quiet soon after.

Adrian stopped breathing. Had he killed it? No, it was still moving, tapping its claws rhythmically against the ground. A painful knot in his stomach came undone. "Anything serious I missed?"

The creature cocked its head to the side, a jerky, mechanical gesture reminiscent of a wind-up toy, and clicked, *Uncertainty. Less-pain.*

All right, time to think about how he was going to move it. Teleporting, both instantaneous Keeper transport or the slower, publicly available version, was off the table. Reality didn't need any more strain to deal with.

He would have to carry his unexpected guest.

"I'm not sure I should move you," he said bluntly. "If I missed something and wind up agitating it, you might die before I can find someone to help you. But I've done all I can, and staying here won't be good for your health. Will it?"

Oil-slick eyes peered up at him. *Discomfort.*

He was going to take that as a "no." "We'll stay here until the pain's faded a bit more. Tell me when you can move."

The creature trilled softly, still gazing at him. Adrian stared back, the adrenaline in his system starting to fade as a familiar, bone-deep weariness came trickling back. He could hear space-time unravelling nearby, but while the noise put him on edge, it wasn't yet unbearable. The hole must be relatively small—probably just big enough for a person to slip through. It would hold for a night while Adrian focused on the injured survivor.

The survivor in question wriggled forward a few inches, bringing itself directly into the puddle of electric light. It made a new sound: a chirp. *Less-pain. Cognition. Confusion-unfamiliarity.*

"I'm not surprised," Adrian said, swallowing a yawn. "I don't think you're from around here."

Confusion. Clawed digits scraped hideously as it edged closer. *Recognition?*

"What do you—?" The words caught in his throat. He'd assumed the resemblance to Leslie came from poor lighting and his own exhaustion, but he knew that face. He'd seen it across from his every day for seventeen years. He still saw it in the mirror every morning. The hair was jet black and longer than he liked to keep his, but it fell the same. The eyes had neither whites nor irises, but the shape was the same. It had the same soft mouth, the same fine cheekbones stretched over a completely inhuman jaw.

It was like staring into a distorted mirror. A distorted twin. Adrian's mouth went dry. "Recognition," indeed.

"Who are you?"

The creature cocked its head to the side, eyes fixed on him. *Uncertainty.*

How convenient. Adrian opened his mouth to demand answers, then stopped. Getting upset was unlikely to solve anything. "You look familiar. Do you know why?"

Uncertainty, it repeated, still staring. It really did look like Leslie right after he'd died.

Adrian gritted his teeth. Those eyes were no less disturbing in the light. Nothing but inky black where the sclera and pupil should be, pierced by a thin ring of silver. At least its forehead was bare. If he saw red bloom under its hairline like a gunshot wound, he didn't know what he'd do. He held the creature's gaze until his eyes watered, but nothing changed. Finally, he shook his head and stepped away.

This wasn't Leslie. Even if it looked like him. Even if this dead and damaged thing might have been Leslie once. There were some things a person couldn't emerge from the same as they'd been before. Death was one of them. No point in projecting his own baggage over this broken body. He needed to keep his head down and do his job.

He had been thinking of Leslie earlier today. This was his curse for dwelling on things he couldn't change.

Confusion, it clicked. *Clarity?*

"It's nothing. I'm just tired."

As soon as the words were out, he regretted them. But the creature only looked at him before grumbling to itself.

Translate-error.

"Maybe. I don't know how we're communicating. I'm going to assume it's based more in concepts than actual words."

The creature's head bobbed, birdlike. *Agreement.*

"No wonder we're having trouble." He sighed. "This is not the place to have this conversation. Do you feel up to being moved?"

Bloodless lips curved in a wide smile, revealing sharp metal spikes in place of teeth. *Uncertainty. Enthusiasm.*

Despite everything, Adrian found his own mouth curving upward in response. After a moment's hesitation, he slid his coat off his shoulders, draping it around narrow shoulders. The creature was built inhumanly thin. It was practically drowned in black fabric.

Confusion.

"In case anyone's watching," he said. "And to catch the drips if you're still bleeding."

It blinked. The movement was slow and even, like the turning of a gear. *Confusion. Acceptance.*

"Good. Let's go."

The creature was much lighter than it looked. Judging by its proportions, it would be as tall as he was standing upright, with the tail adding an additional two meters, but it weighed about as much as a large cat. Was it running on another set of laws of physics, or did it just have a lightweight composition? Who knew? He turned away from the alley and began walking in the direction of home, ignoring the cold oil seeping through his coat.

The creature curled away from the light and buried its face in his shoulder, claws twitching in time with his footsteps.

Adrian held it tighter and began to hum.

This was one of the first spells he'd learned: a perception-blurring effect that removed any sense of urgency in listeners. Didn't matter that the creature's skin was practically glistening under the lamps or that he could feel its claws poking through the layer of fabric, anyone close enough to see them would walk right past. It was a spell kept secret, even within the hidden world, and for good reason. You could get a lot done while the world turned a blind eye. Theresa had been furious to find that he'd learned such an unsavory spell long before he became a Keeper. And yet, when a thread of whalesong rose to twine around the notes, he couldn't bring himself to feel surprised. It wasn't quite the same song, but after a few seconds' experimentation, it settled into a flawless harmony.

Thunder rumbled overhead.

Raindrops began pooling on the street.

Adrian pulled the wrapped body closer to his chest.

It was no good. The cold seeped through his shoes. All the warmth drained out of the world. Time rolled back as an uncanny light pierced the darkness, and for a moment, he saw bloodied blond hair spilling out from under the coat.

The creature slithered partly free from its confinement and chirped worriedly at him. *Awareness?*

"I'm fine." Adrian inhaled sharply, held it for three seconds, then breathed out. "Just bad memories."

From that point on, the creature chirped and trilled near constantly, as if it—like Leslie—refused to be quiet any longer than it had to.

THE RAIN DIDN'T let up, and neither did the unwelcome flashbacks. Adrian's guest had taken it upon itself to keep him from drifting back into his own thoughts. It had succeeded with flying colours. By the time they turned onto his street, he was having trouble thinking of the opinionated bundle of skin, air, and various alloys in his arms as an "it." He didn't want to jump to conclusions, either—he didn't know if assigning a gender to it would be welcome or accurate. He hadn't even determined if it had a name yet. Tentative questioning got him nothing but uncertain hissing. He could, however, pinpoint the exact moment the creature's curiosity had overcome its reluctance to jar its wounds. That was the moment it had decided that holding still was for suckers and Adrian's shoulders looked a bit like a jungle gym. One intense, half-understood argument later, the creature had planted its claws on his shoulders, squirmed around until it could prop itself into something that wasn't quite a standing position, and began examining their surroundings with every sign of enthusiasm.

He rolled his eyes. "Enjoying yourself?"

Curiosity. Confusion-unfamiliarity. Excitement.

It was amazing how much personality could be packed into a jumble of clicks, trills, whistles, and concepts. In the fifteen minutes they'd spent together, Adrian had gotten a better grasp of the creature's character than he had of some people he'd known for years. Most of that had consisted of trying to fight its insatiable curiosity and keeping it from wiggling out of his hold. He'd been so occupied he'd had to stop humming aloud. The perception filter was still playing in the back of his head, an idle, droning buzz that set his teeth on edge, but his spells were always weaker when he wasn't singing or speaking them aloud. More prone to failing.

Curiosity, the creature trilled, coiling its surviving tail around his back for balance as it twisted to peer down the street. *Destination?*

"Yes. I live here." The words were uncomfortable to hear aloud. Adrian lived here, as much as he lived anywhere. He'd spent his childhood homeless and his adolescence constantly on the run. Things had stabilized after he found his way to the Gates, when he began his concerted effort to work himself to death. His apartment was little more than a glorified storage locker. He preferred it that way.

Concern. Hesitation. Suspension-judgement.

"It's not very pretty," Adrian agreed.

The apartments on Terrace Drive had been built in a wealthier climate, when the housing market was booming and the city borders were expanding. Then the bubble crashed in the wake of the Guertena crime family's destruction. A lot of landlords found themselves with properties too large to maintain and too expensive to rent. One by one, they'd left for greener pastures. The few who'd stayed had drastically changed their business models. Stately homes had been broken up into much smaller blocks of apartments. Most had faded paint and a few had boarded-up windows. Three buildings were abandoned entirely, their lawns overgrown and wild; another four were between tenants. The road under his feet was pitted and cracked from the winter snow. The city still hadn't gotten around to repaving.

When the Guertenas owned Terrace, it had been all picture-perfect white paint and balconies cut straight from a magazine. Adrian had hated it. The street had more life to it now. He sort of wished he'd witnessed the transformation himself, but he'd been mourning Leslie—and learning what being a Keeper meant—at the time.

A suspiciously judgmental whir tickled his ear. *Scrapyard.*

"Yes."

Confusion.

"It's easy to hide among the garbage." Adrian had picked the neighbourhood for its available space, the lack of neighbours, and the unspoken agreement that those unlucky enough to end up here wouldn't meddle in each other's business. He rarely wore his professional illusion here, and he hadn't exchanged more than a dozen words with his neighbours since he'd moved in. Most of those had been about the weather—exactly how he liked it.

The creature bent over backward, spine curving like rubber until Adrian's back ached in sympathy. It held that pose, staring into his eyes. Though they had the same face, there was something alien in the way it showed expressions. A certain plasticky stiffness mixed with eyes that didn't move right and a mouth that stretched far too wide. *Confusion. Familiarity.*

"You used to live in a similar place?" That was a funny mental image. For a moment, he considered it: this creature living in an inverted, metallic version of Terrace, sprawled boneless over a rusting steel porch or black rubber sidewalk. Maybe it had curled up behind alien windows the way Leslie used to, playing with blades instead of guns, carrying on a steady stream of commentary about anyone who passed by. That thought carried with it the assumption that, of course, it would have someone like Adrian waiting for it—someone to listen to that chatter, throw in criticisms when required, and stop brewing trouble before it got out of control.

He hoped that, if it did have someone waiting for it, that person took its absence better than he had taken Leslie's. His name hadn't always been Adrian. Changing it had been a survival tactic. After all, the person he used to be had died with his twin.

The creature gave a slow, deliberate shake of the head. Nothing birdlike about this movement. Had it picked that gesture up from watching him? Adrian racked his brain, but he couldn't recall demonstrating the art of shaking one's head "no" to it.

Incorrect. It sneaked another glance down the street, forked black tongue darting out to taste the air. *Other-familiarity.*

What was that sound trying to convey? Nostalgia? Déjà vu? The uncertainty of meeting someone after having a dream about them? All of the above? Adrian tried to untangle the string of ideas into something that made sense. He failed. It was too late in the day for this. Or too early. "Forget it. It can wait until tomorrow."

A thin mouth curled in what might have been a pout. *Acknowledgement*, it trilled, the sound grumpier than it had been before. *Haste. Importance.*

"I said, tomorrow."

Claws tugged at his coat, brushing dangerously close to his throat. A barrier spell leaped to the tip of his tongue. He swallowed it when the creature trilled again, eyes narrowed. *Importance*, it repeated. *Forget?*

Adrian let out a careful sigh, very aware of the slight distance between his skin and those serrated digits. One twitch, and both skin and fabric would shred like butter. "I won't forget. I've got a lot to do tomorrow, so it'll take me a while to get around to it, but I won't forget."

It leaned forward, slick hair brushing his cheeks. The strands felt oddly slippery and left smears of dark fluid where they touched him. *Uncertainty.* A pause. *Cynicism?*

He frowned. "You're not sure I'll remember?"

Another jerky nod. *Other-familiarity.*

"Still not sure what you mean." Adrian had walked this path so many times he no longer needed to pay attention to the route. His feet knew where he was going. "If I don't remember by tomorrow, remind me."

The creature went rigid in his arms.

"Hey, you still there?"

A low, drawn-out whine emerged from its throat, accompanied by a tangle of imagery. Most of it slid through his head without a scrap of comprehension. What little stayed made even less sense. *Negative-limited-time. Negative-quiet.* Its eyes darted around, taking in everything around it. Pavement. Mailboxes. Crumbling brick façades. Everything. *Death? Negative-death? Recognition. Familiarity? Negative-familiarity?*

"Please stop," he groaned. "You're giving me a headache. Simple thoughts."

The creature gave a frustrated click. *Time.*

"Tomorrow," he promised again. "We can sort this out then. Right now, you need to rest."

Accompaniment.

"Yeah, me too."

His building loomed ahead, the spectral orchestra of its magical defences gone silent. The absence sent a prickle of cold down Adrian's spine. He'd never really been young enough to believe in the illusion of safety a home provided, but he had believed in the layers of spellwork he'd built into this place. He'd been certain a nuclear strike could be ordered on the city and his apartment would shake off everything but the smell. And yet his wards had gone down at the same time as everything else. That sure showed him. Hopefully, fixing them would be only a matter of forcing magic back into the system. Rebuilding his wards from scratch would give him too much time to dwell on things that couldn't be changed.

Claws dug into his shoulder as he whistled sharply, drawing out the sound for several seconds, pitch soaring higher like the cry of a hawk. This wasn't an anchored spell in the traditional sense—it fed off itself in a circle rather than sinking into the dirt to slumber. There was no attempt to contain the magic, and thus no confinement to be disrupted. Clumsy spellwork, but it stayed, a phantom whistle going on forever, waiting for someone to dare try and harm those under its protection.

"There we go," Adrian murmured. "You all right up there?"

The creature settled on his shoulders in a boneless sprawl. *Confusion. Destination?*

"This is home. You can rest here." It should be safe to stay the night. Whatever had caused the blackout, the worst of it seemed to be over. Now it was just a matter of finding what had been blown, patching over the holes, and waiting for the local reality to repair itself. Oh, and hunting down whoever was responsible, assuming they'd survived. There were many reasons the Keepers tried to stop people from screwing around with the fundamental forces of the universe. One of them was that it tended to be fatal.

After a bit of encouragement, he managed to get the creature to position itself so that he could get them through the door without bumping into anything. Aside from a few aborted squeezes of its talons, his guest remained still, taking in everything around it with wide eyes. Maybe curiosity or weariness kept it silent, or maybe it was just shocked that Adrian could cast such a clumsy ward while running on fumes and still have the magic last. It wouldn't be the first time someone had frozen upon identifying him as a Keeper.

He dropped the perception filter as soon as they were inside.

The room was dark. Adrian hissed repeatedly as he walked shin-first into confiscated magical artifacts, weaponry, and the assorted miscellany that made their homes on his floor. His guest tried to click warnings. They didn't help. Finally, they reached their destination, an island of usable furniture. One couch was covered in a protective layer of junk; the other, set aside for guests and then never used, was clean aside from a layer of plastic to catch spills. Adrian laid his twitchy burden down on that one. It took what was left of his coat with it.

"Lights?" he asked.

Pain, the creature informed him. *Confusion*.

"Do you want me to turn the lights on?"

A low, electric hum. *Desire. Sight.*

He hummed back, and the light bulbs flickered to life. The creature sank against the cushions and screwed up its eyes like a newborn kitten. For a moment, he was struck with a bone-wrenching sense of familiarity. As if the last eight years had never happened. As if he'd never betrayed his other half. As if he'd never been left alone. He slammed the door on that feeling immediately.

The creature on his couch was its own independent entity. The face it wore meant nothing. Even so, it was difficult to tear his eyes away.

Adrian realized that he'd overestimated the creature's resemblance to humanity. Its smooth, poreless flesh was the dead white of bone and printer paper. Its body was slender, sinuous, and sexless at first glance. A second look revealed that, while it lacked most secondary sexual characteristics, it did appear to have primary ones. Its body, at least, was male, no magic required to ensure that. An old pang of envy rang through Adrian. He and Leslie hadn't been so lucky. Its eyes had a rubbery black around them in place of lashes that magnified their blackness. The rings of silver seemed to serve as irises. They contracted as Adrian watched, but its expression remained blank.

Mostly blank. There was a faintly curious cast to its face that Adrian found unsettling. He was used to being unsettled; he was in the wrong line of work to avoid existential discomfort. But this was…different. Like looking in a funhouse mirror. One full of old memories better left buried.

"Have you picked a name yet?" he asked.

Outside, the rain continued to pour.

Incorrect.

Adrian did not roll his eyes, but it was close. "I need something to call you. And do you have a preferred pronoun? 'It' is rather dehumanizing but is standard procedure when approaching a non-human intelligence."

His guest blinked at him. *Confusion. Pain.*

"Names are important," he insisted. "They really should have been the first thing we exchanged."

Confusion. Identify-sound-subject?

"Yes, names are used as identifiers. They're invaluable when it comes to telling people apart."

The creature cocked its head, inky black strands clinging to its cheeks. *Confusion. Separation-obvious. Identify-sound-unnecessary.*

"Not always," he argued. "In crowds or situations where it's difficult to pick out one person, it's easier to have an individual identifier to address the one you want. The same applies if visibility is limited."

Probability, it clicked. *Limited-circumstances.*

"Wider than you might think." Adrian decided to try another tactic. "Do you know whose face you're wearing?"

The look the creature levelled at him was distinctly unimpressed. *Awareness. Self.*

"It's not your face. Not just your face. Look." He tapped his cheek, drawing the creature's oily gaze. "It's mine, too. It'd be pretty hard for someone to get us confused, but not every pair of lookalikes are lucky that way. We even have a word for people so similar it's practically impossible to tell them apart."

A soft chirrup. *Curiosity?*

"Twin," he said softly. "The word is 'twin.'"

Twin, his guest repeated. It lifted a claw to point at him. *Twin?*

He backed up a step under that oil-slick stare. "No."

Familiarity, the creature argued.

"We're different. I am not your twin."

Confusion. Disgruntlement. Understanding.

Good. "Most of the time, the problem isn't so severe, but it's still helpful to have an additional form of identification. Understand?"

Affirmative, his guest trilled.

"My name is Adrian Somer," he said slowly and clearly. "If you've got a similar identifier, I'd like to know. If you don't, that's fine, but then you're going to get stuck with one I come up with for the foreseeable future."

Comprehension. The next sound it made was a long, drawn-out whistle that rapidly changed octaves and tune. The noise was hauntingly familiar, but Adrian had never heard anything like it in his life. A sound at odd angles with the world, one that fit neatly into a place he hadn't known was empty. Disorienting, but not unpleasant.

His heart sank. The problem with talking to an entity that communicated through magic was that magic was a difficult thing for the human brain to process. Usually, it hitched a ride on a pre-existing sense rather than creating a new one. Adrian was a Keeper, with all the excess power that came with being linked to the Gates, but more importantly, he was an auditory practitioner. His brain was already wired to perceive the unknown through sound, and he had plenty of practice committing spells to speech and music. As long as his guest was broadcasting its intent, he could translate its communications into words. With patience and practice, he *might* be able to replicate that noise. The odds of anyone else being able to, though…

"I'm sorry, but no one else on this plane of existence is going to be able to pronounce that. Do you mind if I give you a nickname?"

The creature tilted its head quizzically. *Short-proximity-identifier?*

"Something like that."

Demonstration-proximity. Bloodless lips peeled back, revealing silvery spikes jutting out of black, rubbery gum. *Approval.*

"Glad the idea meets your standards." He'd like to say he put a lot of thought into choosing his guest's nickname, but it was early, he was tired, the clock on the wall was ticking, and he latched onto the first thing he came up with. "How does 'Whistler' sound?"

Acceptable. Cute.

This time, Adrian did roll his eyes. "Oh, shut up, Whistler."

A round of further questioning and some deliberate examples confirmed that, regardless of Whistler's understanding of gender as a concept, its preferred pronouns were he/him. The reasoning given was as simple as it was disturbing: *Familiarity. Repetition.*

Adrian was ready to demand Whistler put more thought into this when he realized that Whistler wasn't talking about copying him. If Whistler remembered being referred to by those pronouns before, had it been in contact with humans before? Food for thought. In the meantime, it was clear that his guest had no intention of changing its—his—mind. Adrian gave Whistler a searching look before giving in gracelessly. "All right, fine. Tell me if you end up wanting something else."

Agreement. Whistler nestled into the plastic-covered couch and tugged the remains of the coat over his shoulders.

"You okay for now?"

Pain. Confusion.

Adrian scowled. "Are you going to die if I leave you here overnight?"

Negative. That hinged jaw cracked open in a skull-splitting yawn, black tongue worming its way free. *Remember.*

He swallowed an answering yawn and turned away. "I will. Now sleep."

The soft screech of metal sliding on metal and couch springs squealing told him that Whistler was following his advice. Adrian should do the same. But before that, he needed to make some calls.

ADRIAN KEPT A landline because, unlike a mobile phone, it tapped into the privacy wards around the house. He'd never felt a need to augment it specifically, so it was still in working order. Dialing Kade's number took longer than it should have; the labels on the keys kept blurring and jumping around. Focusing on the keypad cleared the first problem up, but not the second. It took him a moment to realize his fingers were shaking.

She answered halfway through the first ring.

"How's your shift going?" he asked.

"Better than it could be," she said. "Fire's dealt with. Casualties are within acceptable limits. We need to bring in a ward specialist or start relocating the entire industrial district."

He sat on the floor and peeled off his shoes and socks. Was he still bleeding? Yes, he was. A few soft, atonal notes dulled the pain.

Kade kept talking. "Whose bright idea was it to seal so many spirits in old warehouses? And who had the bright idea to use magic instead of proper insulation in so many telephone wires? The good news is that no one in particular is being targeted. The bad news is that whatever's going on, it's not only breaking loose every old ghost, inter-dimensional portal, and frozen disaster in town—it's also poking holes in the fabric of local reality. I'd say we have about three days before the whole city finds itself adrift in the multiverse."

Adrian's blood went cold. "What?"

"I said what I said. And I think the dead zone is spreading. Right now, it's still within city limits, but that won't last." A harsh bark of laughter. "We're in trouble, Adrian."

"How are people taking it?"

"Badly."

Adrian let his eyes fall shut and pressed his forehead against the wall. Some practitioners belonged to organizations large and financially stable enough to afford workarounds for disasters. Most of them didn't. "How much of our response infrastructure is still active?"

"The WordWeb went down for a bit. I got it mostly fixed, since it's rooted in living memory rather than anything environmental. Still a bit glitchy, though. Not much else is working." She sighed. "I think I can delay outright panic for a couple days. Any longer and we're looking at a potential exodus."

So, reality failure was imminent, there was a potential magical refugee crisis on the horizon, and the closest thing to supports they had were a confused alien and the magical AI database that called itself the WordWeb.

"They blame us." It wasn't a question.

"Of course they blame us! We're such handy scapegoats."

Adrian sighed again. The Gatekeepers weren't a government or even a law enforcement operation. They were a parks service managing a natural resource, stretched too thin. Even the practitioners who made it clear they intended to mess with the Gates, no matter the consequences, couldn't be monitored for more than a few years. All it took was one person with big dreams and little sense to bring the whole precarious system toppling down.

"We need to get to the bottom of this."

"I know." He glanced back into the living room where Whistler lay motionless on the couch, stray oil pooling on the tarp. "I found something on my walk home. Something alive. I've been calling him Whistler."

A moment of careful silence. "Think there's a connection?"

"It's too soon to rule out any possibilities. But he's been nice enough so far, and he's hurt."

"What is it?" she asked.

"He. I have no idea." Adrian shut his eyes again. "Looks like some sort of robot, but there's a flesh component, and the metal resembles musculature and bone structure. Last time I checked, no one had gotten that far in robotics, inside or outside the hidden world." A moment of hesitation. "And he's wearing my face."

Kade scoffed. "Outside, they're impressed if a robot can walk up and down stairs. The face, though…that's interesting. What do you think, some kind of illusion?"

"It's not an illusion. He's just…my twin. My monochrome, black-eyed, sharp-toothed twin." So close and yet so far from Leslie's blond hair, blue eyes, and sharp-edged smile.

"Sounds neat. How advanced are we talking here, structure-wise?"

"I'm not a mechanic. I can tell you this, though—those injuries were deliberate. Looks like something sawed off half his body. And something was pulled out of his back."

A brief silence. Then she laughed. "Great! So space-time is crumbling around us, the Inside's freaking out, and you've got an injured something-or-other dumped in your lap. Think we can trick some poor sucker into picking up the slack long enough to catch our breath?"

"I'll ask around for you," he said, deadpan. "I'm calling Theresa after this, anyhow."

"Good man. I'll come over and take a look at your find tomorrow, once the usual round of apologies and platitudes is over. Hopefully the old lady will know what it is, but I'll give it a shot if she doesn't."

Adrian made a noncommittal noise. He still wasn't looking forward to introducing her to Whistler. Kade could work a crowd like no one else, but she wasn't always the most delicate.

He'd been quiet too long. A sigh crackled in his ear. "Adrian. Do you think this has anything to do with the Gates?"

"I hope not," he said honestly, "but I'll check tomorrow."

"When are you planning to head out?"

He cracked an eye open experimentally. It felt like trying to lift his own body weight with his eyelid. Weariness muffled his senses and turned his thoughts to molasses. It was rooted in the core of his being, bone-deep and aching, the sort that couldn't be washed away with a night or two of rest. Whatever was going on with Whistler, he wouldn't be putting the pieces together tonight. "Eight, unless something comes up."

"Great, see you around nine. I'll bring a map. Let's hope that playing connect-the-dots makes a pretty picture and we can sleep in the day after, huh?"

Kade hung up without any further pleasantries.

Adrian followed suit, then picked up the receiver again and dialed another number. Eight years ago, an empty shell of a man had stood in front of the Second Gate, frozen with terror and indecision, staring blankly up at something he couldn't comprehend. That hesitation had saved his life. It had given Keeper Theresa Hargreaves enough time to notice him tripping her wards. She'd been the one to find him and guide him away from the lethal defences layered around the Gate. Then she'd laid her coat over his shoulders and tugged him back into reality with her.

When she'd realized how cold he was, she'd taken him straight to the nearest hotel to warm up. When she'd found Leslie's blood on his face, his hands, his shoes, she'd scrubbed it off and watched it swirl down the drain in silence. When she'd figured out who he was—and what he was connected to, what he'd done—she'd just asked him if he wanted to do something good with the rest of his life. He'd nodded, and she'd given him a new name, new records, and something to live for. She'd even helped him finish transitioning magically, the way Leslie had never gotten a chance to. Although he knew the odds of getting in contact with her now, years after he'd set off on his own, were low, something in him relaxed at the thought of hearing her voice.

She didn't pick up. Too busy with her own disasters.

Adrian laid out the facts for her answering machine as calmly and professionally as he could despite the huge yawn in the middle of his explanation. Then, because he'd promised Kade he would, he outlined the gruesome details of what had happened today and asked for assistance that wouldn't come. Finally, he hung up and padded back into the living room.

Whistler hadn't moved. He lay on his stomach, claws tucked under him like a cat, so still that for a second Adrian thought he'd died. But he was breathing, shallow but steady, and no oil marred his slack face. His wounds appeared to be closing; at this rate, the "bleeding" would be over by the time he woke up. If he woke up.

Adrian made his way to the hall closet and extracted a faded quilt. A housewarming gift from Theresa when she'd judged him fully trained and had kicked him out into the world. Sewing had never been her strong suit, but it was still a comfy blanket.

Whistler didn't stir as Adrian laid the quilt over him and left the room.

THE DAY HAD been so terrible that Adrian half expected to see a tracery of silver and spiderweb—or worse, rust and grave dirt—when he closed his eyes. He didn't. Something else was waiting to pounce.

Keepers had an odd relationship with dreams. Some found their slumbering minds restricted to a certain pattern, or they were haunted by oddly specific things. Others were dogged mercilessly by dreams that would not leave them alone. Adrian had never been especially susceptible to prophecies or portents, but Theresa saw visions of possible futures constantly. Kade had told him once, under the influence of grief and too much alcohol, that she hadn't dreamed since she found the Gates. He wished he could say the same.

It started, as always, with the sound of rain tapping against pavement. Slowly, Adrian became aware that he was standing on a street corner. Grease and burnt crust filled his nose when he breathed in. The sky was grey with clouds. A neighbourhood took form around him—a place he'd spent years trying to forget.

Those efforts hadn't been entirely unsuccessful—he could no longer tell how many paces it would take to cross the street, and the buildings were nothing but smears of colour. But they were still arranged in the right order: pawn shop, scuzzy pharmacy, crappy pizza joint, guy who sold weed out his backdoor. The alley was the one thing clearly defined in a land of blurs. Each individual brick stood out clearly, marked with its own pattern of grime. Inside that alley lurked two small figures.

Without looking away, Adrian reached down and pinched himself. It didn't hurt. It didn't feel like much of anything. It certainly wasn't enough to wake him up. Figured. He squeezed his eyes shut and waited. Seconds later, a pair of little footsteps came running out of the alley. They made a sharp turn and scampered onto the sidewalk. A third set of footsteps emerged from the haze of noise, this one much heavier. The slap of thin soles on concrete grew closer and closer to that ponderous tread until all three of them stopped.

Adrian opened his eyes. A pair of little kids wearing grimy jackets stood across from him, frozen on either side of a much bigger silhouette. Unwashed blond hair spilled out of their hoods, not quite long enough to hide the shock on their faces. Each had a hand extended at the level of the silhouette's pockets. Those small hands were being held hostage.

Blurry features stretched in an unpleasant smile. "Hello there, kids."

The kid on the right quailed, shrinking back as far he could. The kid on the left glared up at his captor and tried to pull his arm free.

"Let go," Leslie snapped.

"It was a nice attempt. Your technique could use some work, but your instincts are good."

He huffed. "Don't know what you're talking about."

"I think you do," the silhouette said mildly. "And I think we both know what would happen if I were to report this to the police."

The quiet boy—Adrian, no, back then he'd still been Ashleigh—shrank even farther. Leslie noticed and started spitting fire.

"You don't scare me, jackass! If you were gonna bring the cops in on this, you'd have made a scene." He gave his arm another yank. "You're not gonna call the cops. So let us go or say what you really want!"

A low, rumbling chuckle. "How would you boys like a job?"

Adrian was too far away to see, but he knew both sets of blue eyes had just turned calculating.

"What kind of job?" Ashleigh asked.

"Doesn't matter." The words dragged themselves out of Adrian's throat before the silhouette's mouth began to move. "Don't take it. Just run."

The twins listened, still tense and half waiting for a chance to escape. But they didn't listen to Adrian. They never did. "You want us to steal for you?"

"And a few other things," said the man whose face he'd gone through a lot of trouble to forget. "A distraction at the right time, a pair of sweet little angels to make the person with them seem less suspicious. You understand."

The boys looked at each other. Turned back. Nodded. The figure released their arms and gestured for them to follow. Adrian watched them go—cautiously at first, then more boldly.

"Who are you, anyway?" Leslie asked.

The figure laughed. "Aleister Guertena. Call me Al."

The rain poured down. Adrian's hair was plastered to his skin. He couldn't feel his fingers. Ahead of him loomed something horrible and unnamable. This was the moment his and Leslie's path had been decided. This was the moment his brother's death had been set in motion. In a burst of grief and denial, he bit down on his tongue, severing it.

He woke shaking and terribly alone, the phantom taste of iron thick in his mouth.

IV

SHION WAS DOUBLE-CHECKING the latest glyph stencil when her vision began to blur. She rubbed her eyes, but it didn't help. With a soft groan, she reached for her watch and squinted. Just after eight in the morning. She hadn't slept in over twenty-four hours. Her muscles had gone stiff, and her bones creaked as she slid out of her chair.

Charlie was at her side before she could fall, his big hands around her shoulders. With his help, she stayed upright even as her legs were consumed by pins and needles. "Shion, are you all right?"

"I'm fine," she lied. "Just tired."

He nodded, but the tightness around his eyes didn't ease. There was an uncomfortable tension in the air.

Shion leaned heavily on him while she looked around. The warehouse was once again full of activity. Tina and a few others were erasing unnecessary chalk lines. Soo-bin watched the gauges on the Thaumaturgical Scale. Maria was dashing back and forth across the pattern, noting down every rune that could be removed to save power. The rest of the coven was curled up in fold-out cots, catching up on their sleep.

Another cot, far in the back, held Janine's body. A stasis spell had been erected around it so she wouldn't decay. Though her eyes were closed, her expression was far from peaceful. The resolve on her face was painful to look at.

Shion's eyes skittered off her contorted features and landed on the outer edges of the diagram. "How are we doing for time?"

"Not bad," Charlie rumbled. "We've still got about two-thirds of our power left. Janine only disturbed the chalk, so all we lost was the charge trapped in the upper layers." He nodded toward the stencil on her folding desk. "With these, reapplication should be quick. Question is, how quick?"

They didn't have a lot of time to redo the ritual before someone came poking around. Charlie had been the one to cut a deal with the warehouse's owner, so his concern was rather personal, if silly. This wasn't a repeat of the Guertena affair, when there had been so many people implicated in the attempt to reach the Gates that the Keepers had only sentenced the ones directly involved. Shion's coven was small, and unlike her former employers, she hadn't suckered any of them in under false pretenses. They all knew what they were doing, which made them all equally guilty.

"Don't worry. It won't take long. Two more days at most."

"Two days." The relief in his voice was tangible. "Then the drain will disappear?"

So he was worried about the side effects? Shion hadn't been outside since the initial failure, but she'd heard about the fallout in whispers from Charlie and the others who'd dared venture out with him. Apparently, the city was in a state. It didn't matter to her. Anyone who died could be brought back once her proof of concept was finished and Yves was by her side again. "Yes. It will disappear and we can start bringing everyone back."

"Good. That's good."

She had Charlie. Now to reel him in. Everyone in her coven had joined for one purpose, but the details were just different enough to make memorization tricky. She knew Charlie had lost his daughter. He'd told her stories about the dead girl often enough, but Shion couldn't remember the name he'd used for the life of her. Amanda? Aurora? "Two more days and you'll see your daughter again. I'm sure Maria would love to meet her."

He shuffled his feet, well away from the diagram. "Maria's dad will be coming back too. She'll be busy. I'm not sure she'll have time to meet Audrey."

Audrey. That was it. "Do you intend to cut ties with us once Audrey returns?"

Charlie jolted, panic flaring in his eyes. "Of course not! You— Shion, if it weren't for you, I'd still be mourning my baby girl. You, Maria, Janine…" His voice faltered ever so slightly. "I owe you all so much."

"And I owe you for helping me make this a reality." If she stood on tiptoe, she could pat his shoulder. She did so now, even as her dead lover's face filled her mind. "We're comrades in the fight against death itself. This ritual won't be the end of our coven. I still need to introduce everyone to Yves, after all."

Would Yves be disappointed in her for such blatant manipulation? Shion couldn't make herself care.

Charlie relaxed under her touch. "Looking forward to it. Your boy sounds like a good man."

"He is," Shion said, the pain in her legs fading to a pleasant numbness. "I'm sure he'll love you."

ADRIAN WOKE UP in a cold sweat. His internal clock suggested it might be around eight in the morning—he'd gotten about two, three hours of sleep at most.

No wonder he regretted being awake.

He got up. There was no way he'd get back to sleep after that dream. The first order of business was clothes. He had few good memories attached to suits, but they put him in the right mindset. A suit was the perfect uniform for those who walked with death: morticians, hitmen, government agents, Keepers. He could feel a veil of professionalism settle over him as soon as the tie was in place.

The second, after a full minute spent scowling at his reflection, was an elastic, because his hair now reached below his shoulders. Plenty of men had long hair, he knew. And yet, even years after transitioning, Adrian couldn't shake the certainty that long hair on him looked…girlish. Dysphoria was a subtle, creeping thing compared to most other threats he faced, but it was also only ever a day or so away.

A Keeper's first, involuntary trip to the Gates left a mark. All Keepers had part of them permanently changed. These Gate tokens served as a reminder of what the Keepers were linked to. Some were easy to hide: Kade's white hair, for instance. Others—patches of scales, slit-pupiled eyes, forked tongues—were less so. The advent of body modification, bolder fashions, and cosplay allowed Keepers so marked to walk down the street without risk to themselves or the thin barrier separating the hidden world of magic from the ignorant society Outside, but they still attracted attention.

Adrian's Gate token was far from the strangest, but it was the worst. His hair grew about twenty times faster than usual. If he paid attention, he could actually watch the process. No matter how neat—and *short*—it was in the morning, it would be at least chin length by the end of the day. If he let it grow out for a week, it would be hip length. The mere thought made his skin crawl. He didn't have time to cut it neatly, so he just ran a comb through it and shoved it into a low ponytail as quickly as physically possible.

The creeping discomfort eased. Much better.

The third order of business was to check on Whistler, whose stolen face remained slack and motionless as he approached. His guest didn't appear to have moved during the night, and there were no stains on the quilt.

Adrian whistled softly, trying to imitate Whistler's voice.

Black eyes flew open. *Confusion. Recognition?*

"Hello," Adrian said, keeping his voice even. "Do you remember me? We met last night."

Whistler nodded, the motion noticeably smoother than it had been before, and clicked hurriedly. *Memory-transportation. Pain.*

Adrian couldn't quite conceal a smirk. "The trip here wasn't much fun, was it?"

Agreement. Whistler gazed up at him, sharp features settling into an odd expression. *Recollection?*

The dream tickled at his thoughts, its presence a sheet of cold water pressing on his brain. "Yeah. I remember. You wanted to talk about something."

Recollection! Familiarity. Other-familiarity. Negative-familiarity. Confusion.

The flood of concepts felt like a headache given sound. "Too much at once," he said through gritted teeth. "Slow down."

The barrage dwindled to a trickle of something that was difficult to sum up in a single word. Second-hand grief, perhaps. A soul-splitting pain experienced without context or meaning. Loss that would destroy if one only understood what it was. All of that, with a side of misfortunate déjà vu: the feeling you got when something you'd known would happen, but hoped wouldn't, played out exactly as you expected it to. At least, that was the closest equivalent Adrian could think of. It was tempered by confusion, like everything his guest said, but the edges being softened did little to take the sting out.

"You think we've met before."

Other-familiarity. Negative-familiarity.

"We've met before, but you weren't yourself. We weren't ourselves." Adrian was aware his tone was growing sharp, but there was little he could do to stop it. "You're wrong."

Forget, Whistler trilled. *Other-familiarity.*

Adrian remembered that trill. Its contents were less easy to place. A feeling of smallness, the action of looking up, a sense of not being alone, and an impression of anguish stood out to him, but there was more packed in—an entire lifetime, perhaps. A short one, spent doing other people's dirty work, haunted by anger and frustration. Toothy grins. The impulse to start fires just to see what would happen. The certainty that the two of them would never, ever be left alone. These scattered pieces didn't feel like Whistler's memories, but they didn't feel stolen, either. They were too close to the core of who Whistler was, leaking through every time he opened his mouth.

Pieces of Leslie clinging on as junk data. Leftovers from a man—a boy, really—who had been converted into an unrecognizable form. It was a bit of a leap of logic, but it fit uncomfortably well. No wonder Whistler thought he recognized Adrian. They'd been brothers once.

Adrian didn't deserve to be Leslie's brother any longer.

He rubbed his temples, leaning over so he could check the analog clock in the kitchen. Like the landline, it had been deliberately left unenchanted and was still ticking merrily away. 8:45 a.m. He looked down, meeting his guest's uncanny gaze. "I don't have a lot of time. This may not be the best chance to have an in-depth conversation."

Acknowledgement. Desire-recollection.

"You just want me to remember?"

Another creaky nod. *Miscommunication. Difficulty. Pain?*

It took Adrian a second to realize where that last question was directed. Then he laughed, surprised. "No, I'm fine. Just tired."

A skeptical look. Or possibly a "politely refraining from calling you out on your nonsense" look. Either way, Whistler wasn't quite able to capture the expression he was going for. His eyes weren't mobile enough in their sockets and his jaw wouldn't push out far enough. The result was a ghoulish stare. Adrian suppressed a shudder. Showing fear had only encouraged Leslie when he was alive; Adrian doubted it would be any different now that Leslie was dead.

Assuming Whistler was still "Leslie." Selfishly, Adrian hoped he was. He shouldn't. God willing, Whistler was his own person, divorced from everything Ashleigh and Leslie Richter had been.

Concern.

"Stop that. You're the one hurting here." Adrian would be fine. There was always something more important to focus on than the past. Besides, it wasn't like talking about what he'd done would change anything. Some sins couldn't be erased. You just had to live with them. "I need to ask you some questions, actually. Do you know where you are?"

A low hum. *Uncertainty. Familiarity.*

So, mostly no. "Do you know how you got here?"

Confusion. Unclear.

"You can't remember?"

Negative. Unclear, Whistler repeated, stressing the last concept.

"Ah. You're not sure what happened."

Affirmative. Fast. Open-tear. Fall.

Adrian breathed out slowly. "Lucky. Not many would survive falling through a rift like that."

Survival-uncertainty, Whistler grumbled to himself. *Death-uncertainty.*

He wasn't even sure if he was dead? That, Adrian chose to ignore in favour of bringing up his most important question. "Did you see the Gates?"

Whistler's head snapped toward him. *Awareness. Confusion. Affirmative.*

"…do you feel the Gates even now?"

Affirmative.

A tight knot formed in Adrian's chest. In a way, this was good. A new Keeper surviving was always a Godsend. At the same time, he couldn't make himself feel happy for reasons that had nothing to do with Whistler's inhumanity. It was easier to pretend the sudden churning of his gut stemmed from looking too long at the hollowed-out wounds on his guest's back.

"I see," he said finally. The words came out too sharp. "Welcome to the team, then. Wish I had an introductory pamphlet to give you. But I guess you already know the drill."

No one could be drawn to the Gates naturally without understanding what the Keepers stood for. No one except Whistler, who tilted his head nearly 90 degrees and clicked with nothing but confusion. *Purpose. Elaborate?*

"It's simple. The Keepers exist to save the world." That wasn't quite truthful. It implied that the only thing in danger if the Gates were breached was this little ball of water and dirt. So much more was at stake, but hell, "save the world" sounded so much neater. "Save everything—literally *everything*" didn't have the same ring.

Whistler's plastic brow creased. *Protect-Gates. Misconception?*

"That's the most important part of our jobs. If we didn't stand between the Gates and the rest of existence, there wouldn't be a rest of existence." Adrian looked down and flexed his hands, absently calling power to them until his fingertips glowed. "To that end, we're given power. Endless power. It's still barely enough to hold this hidden world together." That earned him a curious click from Whistler, so he expanded. "Most practitioners use magic. We *are* magic, just like the Gates are magic. No matter what, we're going to be stronger than everyone else, so when we fail, we're feared and blamed and spat on. Which doesn't exactly encourage us to do our best at this whole 'protecting reality' thing, and so it repeats."

Unfortunate.

"Yeah," Adrian agreed. "You could say that. I'm doing an awful job of selling you on this. How about we find a way for you to go back wherever you came from and never speak of this again?" He was only half joking. Sending Whistler back might not be possible, and it was a distant priority compared to containing the situation, but it was still on the list. He wanted to make sure Whistler knew this. Most people, stranded in an alien world, would want to return. Though Whistler hadn't exactly been eager to bring up the subject.

Was he a refugee? Adrian didn't know.

Agreement-amusement. Priorities. Whistler pushed away from the cushions and sat up, quilt tumbling down his thin shoulders. *Familiarity? Recollection?*

Adrian's snappish response was thoroughly derailed by the metal spires protruding from Whistler's shoulder blades. He was sure those hadn't been there before, but they fit nicely into the gouges.

Well, when in doubt and in need of a change of subject, ask. "What are those?"

The appendages in question twitched. Whistler cocked his head, the picture of innocence. *Self.*

Adrian assumed that meant they were supposed to be there, implying a rate of healing that was both reassuring and uncanny. "You're regenerating?"

Bloodless lips curved in a wide smile. *Mending!*

Mending? That was an odd choice of word. Adrian straightened and walked around the couch for a better look. The tape was definitely displaced, but there was something different about the metal underneath. It was smoother. Shinier. Like new. "Should I take the tape off?"

Whistler paused, holding his head at an awkward angle, then gave it a firm shake. *Negative. Time?*

Adrian glanced back at the clock and grimaced. He should really keep the conversation going. Leaving an untrained Keeper alone was asking for trouble. But Whistler had been cooperative, and Adrian had no time to spare and no desire to discuss what he'd done to Leslie. Maybe it would be easier for him to face Whistler if he worked himself into an exhausted stupor first. "Thanks. Stay put—you're still a wreck. Don't do anything while I'm not here. Anything you need before I head out?"

Recollection.

He sighed. "I'll try."

Dismay. Acceptance. Whistler blinked slowly, irises swelling in size until his eyes were mostly silver. *Hunger?*

"That depends. What do you eat?"

Whistler began to hum. Flickers of emotion and sensation brushed against Adrian's mind, refusing to solidify into anything concrete. He edged backward, just in case. Whistler didn't seem to notice. Finally, the hum settled into a new sound: a metallic clang, like a pair of spoons hitting each other.

"You eat metal?" Adrian shouldn't have been surprised. Demi-humans and extra-dimensional entities often had major dietary changes compared to regular humans. Odd allergies, expanded palates, and he wasn't going anywhere near the ghoul disaster. That was one hornet's nest no one in their right mind would poke. But…eating exclusively metal? That he'd never heard of before.

Whistler clanged again, flooding Adrian's mind with the clatter of spoons.

"I'll see what I can do." There weren't any large reserves of scrap metal on hand, but half of being a Keeper was taking what you had and improvising. There was a department store within walking distance, and Adrian didn't like any of his utensils anyway.

ADRIAN SHOULD CHECK the place he'd found Whistler. A portal between worlds, even an accidental one, was always worthy of investigation; given the timing, he needed to go over the alley with a fine-toothed comb. But an ounce of prevention was worth a pound of cure, and the Gates came first. Always. Adrian headed downtown instead, skipping the professional illusion as usual. More roads were closed-off than not. The pavement was pocked or chewed up in places. He caught another living sinkhole on the way, this one barely big enough to swallow a bicycle, and trapped it in a bubble of stopped time. The worst of the damage had already been dealt with, but that meant it was time to deal with everything else. Everywhere he looked, the burnt-out husks of apartment buildings loomed overhead. Cars were parked everywhere they could fit with whole families inside. Overhead, power lines crackled with sparks.

Adrian stopped the errant current and cleared away the rubble as he went, searching for a place where the fabric of reality was a bit thicker. When the pressure finally shifted, he paused and took a moment to collect himself.

He didn't want to do this. It was probably unnecessary. The odds that someone had figured out how to slip past the wards set up by generations of Keepers were low, to say the least, but so what? Probabilities were meaningless in the face of reality. If something had gone wrong, no combination of numbers would change that. The only way to make sure the Gates weren't being tampered with was to go and see for himself.

It would turn out fine. Even if Adrian succumbed to temptation, the labyrinth of wards erected by Keepers throughout history would prevent him from doing something irreparable. And yet the idea of going back there—of facing the Second Gate again—terrified him. The sun was up and shining, but the wet slap of rain on concrete echoed in his ears.

He'd put this off long enough. Time to stare into the void and see what looked back.

Keeper transport was one of the few spells it was relatively safe to use publicly in Outside spaces. Ironically, it drew less attention from civilians than from other practitioners. A standard perception filter came as part of the package, taking care of mundane observers, but tearing a hole in the world was the sort of thing a practitioner noticed. Even if the Keeper wasn't currently a cloaked shadow, it was obvious what spell had been cast. Adrian breathed in sharply and let his eyes fall shut. Then, very deliberately, he relaxed his grip on reality. The noise of the crowd faded, replaced with an eerie stillness.

The first step he took, uncertain, was surrounded by red-tinged light. The second step, surer, carried him into darkness. The third step, silent, brought him back into light. Not the light of the sun. Compared to the Gates, the sun was nothing.

Slipping out of reality wasn't supposed to be this easy. It probably hadn't been, the first time he'd stumbled his way to the place between, but all that remained of that night was cold and rain. The details had blurred into whispers, grief, and a sense of awful knowing.

Shock, tragedy, purpose: that was how a Keeper was made.

He opened his eyes. A fathomless darkness surrounded him, stretching out into infinity. There was nothing above him. There was nothing beside him. There was nothing beneath his feet. But in front of him, the First Gate blossomed. It was woven from strands of silver and spiderweb, each thread casting a soft light into the dark. The air around it stirred with every breath ever taken. Faint whispers emanated from the structure, forming words. Adrian let them pass over him without listening. Most were in languages he couldn't understand; all were devoid of context. They'd been pouring out into the universe far longer than he'd been alive. He began to walk, careful not to think too hard about what he was walking on.

The Gate remained where it was, but the puddle of light it cast began to swell. It left no searing streaks in his vision. This was not a light perceived with one's eyes. A sudden clamour hit as soon as he touched it. Thousands of songs played over each other, turning into raw noise in their struggle to be heard. He glanced down reflexively and saw them: diagrams etched at the foot of the gate, splashes of colour and raised surfaces that meant nothing to him. Old magic that predated human history and might well predate humanity. Odd scents that made his eyes water, tastes so hopelessly alien he could only perceive them as pain—layers upon layers of protections that had all failed.

Adrian jerked his eyes up and moved into the darkness beyond. As soon as he was over the threshold, it was pierced by a new light. The Second Gate did not shine silver. There was nothing of the First Gate's ethereal delicacy to be found in its construction. This Gate was forged of bone and rusting metal, hinges molded from grave soil. Shadows and cold wrapped tenderly around its columns, holding the structure together. Radiating from it came chill, the sweet scent of rot, and stark white light.

It was closed. It had always been closed. If the Keepers had their way, it would always be closed.

He braced himself and stepped forward. The moment his toes

touched this light, he was assaulted by a mass of distorted sound far more intense than what he'd endured at the previous Gate. The sheer force of it made him stumble. He didn't bother trying to cover his ears. It wouldn't help. His senses grew more confused as he continued, building until his throat was burning and his eardrums felt ready to burst. One final step took him to the foot of the Second Gate. The onslaught cut out as quickly as it had begun. An inexperienced visitor might assume they'd found a blind spot in the wards. Adrian knew better. There was no place more secure than this.

His breath fogged in front of him. He rubbed his hands together and ran a practised eye over the Gate. The patterns of rust were undisturbed, the shadows hadn't gained any ground, and the sharp-edged bones remained where they had lain for as long as he could remember. His eyes lingered on the structure, black on white on rust on grey. The twisting metal spires, the blood-soaked earth…they called to him like family. Like the only family he'd ever had. Even as the thought crossed his mind, cold seeped into his lungs, carrying with it the scent of decay.

Every time he came to the Gate, he was overwhelmed with the certainty that he wasn't alone in this place. His other half was here. While he'd screamed and cursed and mourned, Leslie had been right here. Waiting. Always waiting.

The rain was still pouring down. He could feel it on his skin, his hair, his clothes. There was blood on his face. His hand had long since gone numb around the gun. Soft whispers drifted toward him, murmuring wordlessly. They were calling his name.

Ashleigh, they sighed, over and over in a thousand voices he couldn't place, though they were so familiar it brought tears to his eyes. *Ashleigh*.

For a moment, a boy who'd died eight years ago drew breath. All that Ashleigh Richter had ever lost was clustered behind that Gate, but his twin was the only one that mattered.

All he had to do was reach out and—

But that wasn't his name anymore, was it?

Adrian Somer froze, fingers centimetres from the Gate. He backed away slowly, heart in his throat. One more second, and those spells would've snapped into action. He could've died, and he hadn't even noticed. Hadn't even cared. Bile rose in his throat. Eight years as a Keeper and he was still so, so weak. Still trembling at the thought of being able to see his brother again. Even though what remained of his brother was probably sleeping on his couch.

How stupid. What was dead was dead. Even if something had brought Leslie back through the Gate, no spell would erase what Adrian had done.

Something appeared in his peripheral vision as he turned away: a small, triangular void. A hole in the pattern where none should be. It took him a few seconds to comprehend what he was seeing. One of the bones that formed the Gate had cracked open, some-thing simultaneously dark and bright seeping out. It smelled like rot and drying blood. It sounded like whispers and the rasp of steel. It looked…familiar, yet unfamiliar. Adrian was profoundly grateful he hadn't been close enough to touch the stuff. Or worse, taste it. He squeezed his eyes and retraced his steps on shaking legs.

Reality settled back over him. Sound came back first, as always; he could have cried when the roar of concentrated spells died away and was replaced by the entirely mundane roar of a crowd. One by one, his other senses exploded into being, but hearing domi-nated. Footsteps, car alarms, the buzzing of insects. The symphonic rumble of power running through a thousand slap-dash spells. A chorus of discordant notes representing a million tiny holes in the world. Adrian opened his eyes just in time to walk into someone. Her signature was marked by blaring synthesizers—a strong mind, loud enough to stick out to his raw senses, but not a magical one. A businesswoman on her way to work.

She turned on him, lips twisted in the beginnings of a snarl, then stopped. "Are you okay?"

He ducked his head, murmured an apology, and fled before she could say anything. The sun was much brighter than it had been when he left. Judging by its position, he'd lost about an hour. His hands were shaking, he couldn't feel his fingers, and he looked bad enough to stop complete strangers in their tracks.

And people *wondered* why the Keepers wouldn't let them use the Gates.

Autopilot had him ducking out of the street and into the shadow between buildings. The cacophony followed him. His senses were still raw. He propped himself up against the wall and dug into his pocket, fishing out a pair of earbuds. The device in his pocket was horribly outdated, but he only needed one song. Visual practitioners like Kade would be able to overcome the effects of Gate exposure with a few scribbled lines. Everyone else had to prepare their stabilizing spells in advance. In his case, that meant music: spells sung in his own voice, played loud enough to drown out the whispers. Loud enough to anchor him to the man he'd chosen to be. He let his eyes slide shut and sank into the recording.

Someone hadn't listened to the warnings. Someone had tried opening the Gate. Now there was a hole in the barrier between reality and what was popularly theorized to be *death*. Something about that image tickled Adrian's memory. He fumbled with the Walkman, turning the volume as high as it would go. He couldn't drown out the noise, but he could cover his ears and try to focus. What about that cracked bone had felt familiar?

Pinpricks of pain danced over his skull. This wasn't working. All he could hear over the music was the distant sound of reality shredding to pieces. It was so loud he almost missed Kade's arrival.

"Hey, Adrian. You're looking well."

He cracked open an eye and grimaced. The world was too bright. "You have glitter in your hair."

"Scared people throw wild parties. And last night, I went where the scared people were." Kade gave her head an irritable shake, scattering points of light everywhere. "I took the bus out here. Bad idea. You're lucky you can't see what this looks like. It's nauseating."

"You're lucky you can't hear what it sounds like," he rasped.

"Yeah, yeah. I've got a few more places to hit before we go back to your apartment. Tell me what you've found on the way."

"There's a crack in the Second Gate."

"You're kidding." Kade gave him a sidelong glance, clearly expecting a smile or a laugh. The seconds stretched out around them. "You're not kidding."

He shook his head.

She swore loudly and pressed her face into her hands. "How are we all even here if it's open?"

"Not open, cracked. There's a hole in it. Something's dripping through. More importantly, someone broke into the Gate from outside, and we had no idea."

"Okay! So we're only slightly before the end of the world instead of directly on top of it!"

"It's not the end," he said, tongue thick and clumsy in his mouth. "We can still stop this."

Kade lowered her hands at last. "We'd better stop it. Damn, no wonder reality's breaking under its own weight." A deep sigh. "All right, let's get this over with. Time to hit the club."

Adrian grimaced and detached himself from the wall. "You're doing the interviews."

"Naturally."

Belle Noise stopped serving alcohol at 2 a.m. but wouldn't close until 10 a.m. That gave the two of them half an hour to sift through the patrons. According to Kade, it was a decent afterhours club: nice atmosphere, good food, decent company. Adrian hated it. It reminded him too much of places the Guertenas had frequented— places he'd once been obliged to waste hours at.

The lights were down. Some enterprising electrician had jury-rigged a replacement, but the strobe effects and bright colours were non-functional. The owner had dimmed the remaining lights, dumped a ton of sparkles on the floor, and called in some local groups to provide live music. It was probably meant to give the club's clientele a distraction from their troubles. In practice, it gave them more shady corners to whisper in.

Kade was in her element, gliding between the bar and groups of frantic dancers with practiced grace. Her reflection showed a woman with a sandier skin tone than Kade's deep brown, much less striking hair, and a softer smile that showed less teeth. It made her look downright approachable. Adrian didn't appreciate it. He wrapped his perception filter around himself and lurked in the corner, trying to block out the pitter-pat of racing hearts and the clamour of a hundred magical signatures playing on top of each other, while she wheedled, coaxed, and commiserated with everyone in sight. Finally, she left the floor and loitered by the bar for a few minutes, where a small East Asian man in rumpled clubwear walked up behind her. She nearly put his eye out with her elbow. Seconds later, they were laughing like old friends. They had one drink each, toasted each other, and then Kade slid off the barstool and headed for the door.

Adrian followed.

The second they were outside, Kade's reflection vanished as the tattooed whorls of her perception filter bloomed into view on her shoulder.

"Well?" Adrian asked.

"Three leads. Two I picked up before this, one new. Charlie Detlaff. Janine Miller. Shion Matreva. Heard of them?"

The answer should have been no. Adrian wasn't exactly a social butterfly, and people didn't like to talk to Keepers who didn't bother with concealing their identities. But something about that last name niggled at him. "Last one's familiar."

"I'm not surprised. Apparently, she lived here a few years back before she got herself arrested. By us. She's still on our watch list."

His train of thought came to a screeching halt. "What for?"

"Before my time. The way I was told it, she made us an offer about the Gates she thought we couldn't refuse. Turned out we could and did. It's a common story, except for the part where she came back after she was released from custody."

"What was she working on?"

"Hell if I know. WordWeb probably has it." The look Kade gave him was somewhere between pleading and plaintive. "You mind?"

He scowled back. "You need to get over this phobia eventually."

"It's not a phobia. I just don't like having something that was never alive rooting around in my head."

This was why Adrian was leery about bringing Kade back to see Whistler. But there was no time to argue about it now. "Fine. Hang on for a second."

He led them down a side street first. Once they were safely out of the way, he turned to face the wall and began to hum a sharp, mechanical tune in a minor key. The WordWeb began to stir, slowly at first, then faster, like an old, creaking mechanism beginning to turn. As it grew louder, Adrian could hear the faint abnormalities in the magic that held the construct together. Those sour notes worried him.

Finally, there was an answering murmur. *'identifier?'*

"Gatekeeper. Adrian Somer," he said, pouring as much of himself as he could into those three words. If the WordWeb broke down…

'accepted,' a voice that was not a voice whispered. *'welcome, keeper somer. would you like to enter?'*

"Yes." A thin layer of power surrounded him. The first and only time Kade had used the WordWeb, she'd described its inbuilt barrier as looking like a soap bubble. All Adrian had to go by was the subtle way it distorted the sound outside it. Even the worst ethereal shrieking became blurred and indistinct. He sat down carefully, keeping his eyes shut. Around him, reality ground against itself like the grinding of clockwork. Every crunch sent chills down his spine. The transfer to the WordWeb's pocket dimension took seconds, but it felt longer.

Finally, the grinding stopped. A chime rang out.

'welcome to the WordWeb, keeper somer. are you searching for something?'

"Yes." Adrian opened his eyes. An endless sea of quicksilver surrounded him, flickers of lettering ghosting beneath its surface. "First keyword—Second Gate. Second keyword—hole, crack, damage. Limitation—spell, ritual. Begin search."

'acknowledged.'

The ocean began to ripple. Columns of glowing text rose around him. Adrian started going through the results as soon as the first one appeared. Spell after spell swam past, accompanied by descriptions of the effects and the required preparations. Some had been added by independent practitioners; others belonged to various cabals and corporations—or would have, if they'd been approved. Anything that came close to the Gates had to pass by the Keepers first. It was a slow, frustrating process for everyone involved. The only thing worse was when someone tried to bypass it. Yesterday and today were proof of that.

Freeware spell that teleported small objects through the space between—approved with modifications.

Corporate spell that siphoned power from the Gate's protections for use in manufacturing—refused, organization placed under observation.

Independent spell, theoretical, intended to change the colour of metaphysical structures to neon purple—refused, inventor offered employment.

Adrian kept looking. Finally, he found something that fit.

Independent spell, theoretical, intended to access an extra-dimensional target directly.

It was flagged for the higher echelons of the Keepers' watch list. He pulled it from the sea of text and began to read.

This ritual, which needed enough energy to drill a hole through the Earth's mantle, was meant to form a portal directly to the Second Gate. There, the caster would crack the seal open, capture some of the energy that leaked out, and use it to "restore biological functions" to a deceased individual. A lengthy thesis was attached in which the spell's inventor argued that the afterlife was located on the other side and that drawing on its power would let her summon the souls of the departed into waiting bodies.

An additional postscript had been added by the Keeper who'd taken her in—a quick look revealed it had been Theresa, in the same year she'd taken him on as a student—outlining the potential side effects. They included localized reality damage, changes in how magic functioned in the affected area, and a risk of breaking the Gate wide open, thus causing the end of the world as they knew it. That danger didn't seem to have occurred to the inventor, who hadn't even bothered to mention how she'd close the hole in the Gate once it was open or how she'd find the right souls. She'd said nothing about what would happen if whoever was resurrected was no longer the same person, either. The wording was eloquent, the subject clearly heart-felt, but the proposal was... telling. He scrolled all the way to the end for the inventor's name, ignoring the icicles forming in his chest cavity.

Now he remembered Shion Matreva.

"Save. Give me a shortcut, too."

'acknowledged'. the WordWeb murmured. *'would you like to make another search?'*

"No. I'm leaving now."

'acknowledged.' The spell he'd been looking at poured itself back into the ocean. He shut his eyes just before the grinding started again. *'goodbye, keeper somer. thank you for using the WordWeb.'*

"You're welcome," Adrian said softly. The barrier went down when the grinding stopped, plunging him back into the maelstrom of noise. His head began to pound in rhythm.

"Well?" Kade asked, leaning up against the brick wall. There was a subtle discomfort in the way she held herself, but most of the tension had gone out of her shoulders. "What else does the data ghost have on her?"

He took a moment to collect his thoughts, steering them carefully away from chilled steel and graveyard dirt and that awful, sucking hole in the universe. "Shion Matreva was a researcher. Worked for a little start-up that was trying to create reliable, mass-produced medication. Pills that would ward off the common cold, seals to keep splints and bandages in place for ages—basic stuff, but on a wide scale, marketed to both the Inside and Outside. It seemed pretty harmless, so nobody poked too deep. Then the Guertenas went down."

Kade's breath hissed out between her teeth. "That was some nasty business."

There was a studied cast to her bland expression, a tense edge to her nonchalant tone. Adrian didn't know why, and he wasn't going to ask. Before their ill-fated grab for the Gates and subsequent destruction, the Guertena crime family had touched a lot of lives, never for the better. "I was called right before the Guertena affair, so I was still in my apprenticeship," he said. "I don't know exactly what happened, but someone found out the firm had serious connections to the Guertenas and the whole thing collapsed overnight. Shion and her partner, Yves Saunders, weren't implicated in any of their employers' crimes. Brilliant couple. Shocked to find out who had been funding their experiments."

"I see," Kade hummed. "How'd Matreva end up on the watchlist, then?"

"Yves died."

"How?"

"I wasn't there," Adrian cautioned. "I was in a hotel room recovering from my first trip to the Gates. I heard after that one of the family's higher-ups broke into their house to silence them both.

Shion wasn't home. The place was warded against magic, but not against bullets."

Kade lowered her head. "That sucks."

"Amazing how many practitioners die by gunshot," Adrian said blandly. "The culprit was jailed and the whole thing was mostly forgotten until a year later, when she approached us with a proposal. She'd designed a ritual. One that required about three times the energy it's safe for independents to screw around with—more than enough to level the city. Her goal was obvious. She wanted to make a portal directly to the Second Gate." He sighed. "She theorized that the afterlife was located on the other side, and that if she drew on its power, she could summon the souls of the departed into prepared vessels."

Dark eyes widened. "She wanted to overwrite peoples' souls?"

"No, part of the ritual would build new bodies. If she'd been actively planning murder, we wouldn't have left her alone." A lot of people thought using the power of the Gates in their research was a good idea. In a better world, the Keepers would have the manpower to filter the genuinely dangerous applications from the half joking or merely oblivious. In this case, Shion had been watched for a while to make sure she didn't try anything stupid, but within a year a catastrophic seal failure had nearly wiped out the East Coast, and a lot of lesser matters had slid to the wayside. Shion had slipped through the cracks, and Adrian had forgotten the whole sad tale. Until now.

Part of him ached with envy. It was easy to say you loved someone enough to sacrifice anything for them. Walking the walk was harder. Adrian could never have done what she had, but for a moment, he wished he could have.

"I see." The tension leaked back out of Kade's shoulders. Part of it, anyways. "So, what were the projected side effects? Somehow I doubt punching a hole straight through to the Gates would go unnoticed."

"Strain in the fabric of reality, holes in local space-time, bizarre consequences for using magic in the area, and a potential for the catastrophic restructuring of the universe."

"Exactly what's happened here, with a bonus in the form of 'bizarre consequences'…" Kade hummed, making finger quotes in the air. "Think the Drain falls under that umbrella?"

Adrian gave her an odd look. "The what now?"

"The Drain! That's what the hidden world is calling this. 'Cause, you know, every disaster these days has to get a badass nickname. Can't just go calling it a blackout or something. That would be silly."

"Yeah, probably. The ritual's details are stored in the WordWeb—I brushed up on them, and I suggest you do the same. Shion is an auditory caster, but she estimated she'd need at least twelve more practitioners to pull it off, so she incorporated aspects of visual and touch-based magic. You'll probably get more out of the records than I did."

"Probably." Kade made a face. It did little to hide how wide her eyes had gone. She cracked her knuckles, and that seemed to steady her. "All right. Daylight's burning. Whatever else you're sitting on, it's time to bring it up."

That was the opposite of what Adrian wanted to do. But he'd already weighed his own desires against the world and found them wanting. "It's Whistler—my guest. If he's connected to the holes and connected to the Gates, then…he's probably connected to Shion Matreva as well."

"So what? You already said you think he was dragged here as a side effect."

Adrian closed his eyes. "Shion wasn't just trying to reach through dimensions. She was trying to bring back the dead. And Whistler…" He shook his head. "I'll know after I see him again. But I think I'm going to have to borrow your eyes."

Kade planted her hands on her hips and snorted. "You Goddamn drama queen. I already agreed to take a look at it tonight, didn't I? We're gonna look for the hole it came through, anyway. How about you just share the ritual details while we're on the move?"

"*He* is going by Whistler. And fine." Adrian pulled his jacket tighter around himself and set off at a brisk walk.

"Whoops, and all right! Lead the way." She followed. After a moment, she started whistling to herself. The manic cheer running through her voice rubbed him the wrong way, but he set the frustration aside. They had work to do.

THE WALK WAS long and arduous, each step bringing a new set of howling tears in the world to Adrian's attention, but the unpleasantness of the walk had nothing on the destination. Last night, the alley had been an oversized rathole. By daylight, it was worse. Flattened garbage bags lay at the foot of a rusting dumpster, contents scattered across the pavement. Refuse blended with scraps of what looked like skin. Layers of stains had soaked into the ground, topped with a puddle of the thick black oil Whistler bled. Something had died in a dark corner; the alley reeked of rot. The air screamed as space and time twisted like a newspaper shredded in the wind. Adrian didn't cover his ears as he entered. It wouldn't help.

Kade lingered at the alley's mouth. "This the place?"

He nodded. He couldn't have mistaken it for anywhere else. Whistler's calls were still trapped in the brickwork. They wove into his thoughts, sharp and desperate and cold, harmonizing with the eerie song of the Gates that never truly left his head. With each ghostly wail, his heart sank further. Finally, he turned away and began listening for the portal specifically.

Where—?

There. Under the clicks and the wails and the shriek of metal lay the sourest notes he'd ever heard. They sounded nothing like nails on a chalkboard or a cat being stepped on, but they set his teeth on edge the same way. Something that had been whole being slowly shredded—that was as close as he could get to describing it. *Thank God for that*, he thought, and waved. "Found it."

Kade's skirt wasn't long enough to swish properly as she picked her way over. Hell if she didn't try, though. Then she got close enough to see what he was listening to, and the sway of her hips came to an abrupt stop. "Oh, gross."

"What does it look like?" he asked.

"An infected wound. The edges are broken somehow. Don't think space-time is supposed to bend that way. Whoever made this had no idea what they were doing. That, or they were out of their mind."

"Artificial, then."

"Definitely," she agreed. "If this is a natural occurrence, I'll eat my shoes."

"Anything else?"

"Yeah. There's…" She tried on and discarded a wide variety of expressions, each of which presumably failed to express the depth of her horrified disgust. "Some kind of discharge."

Alarm bells began ringing. "Details."

"It's—greenish? No, yellowy. No, actually—ugh!" She rubbed her eyes and glared into space. "It's one of those stupid colours that isn't actually a colour. I think it's most like that fuzzy not-grey you get behind your eyes when you stand up too fast."

For a visual practitioner, new colour equalled new magic. Given what they'd just figured out, this shade had horrifying implications.

"It's not oozing, at least. Looks like bits are flaking off, though." Kade sighed. "Somehow I doubt that's any better."

Adrian replayed that last sentence in his head while his scowl deepened. "Flaking off how?"

"In chunks. Layers of stuff peel away from the whole, then crumble away in little pieces."

"Like rust?"

She nodded. "A lot like rust."

How familiar. "How do you think it got here?"

"Gonna go out on a limb and guess that our caster decided to punch their hole through reality somewhere out of the way so no one would stumble into it. Probably had some kind of surveillance set up so they could see what came out. When they saw your guest was useless…" A careless shrug. "Poor little alien left bleeding in an alley. He does have blood, right?"

"Injured. Not useless." Adrian set his jaw and moved toward the noise. "You think this could go two ways?"

"No way in hell. It's bad enough as-is. We open it any farther, we'll send the whole neighbourhood crashing into existential limbo." She shivered, rubbing her bare arms. "Haven't seen anything this bad before."

"I have." Adrian closed his eyes and breathed in. For a moment, the alley became a basement, and it was blood that filled the air. Blood and the sound of rain. That awful, discordant noise of fraying space had been present then, too. He would've done anything to make it stop. And he had.

"Where?" Kade asked, a note of suspicion entering her voice.

"The Guertenas," he said, eyes still shut. "Do you know why the Keepers finally decided to wipe them out?"

"Do I have to? It's the same story. Somebody wanted to open the Second Gate and wouldn't take no for an answer."

"You make it sound so simple. But I guess it always seems simple from the outside."

"Adrian, don't tell me—"

"I was raised by Aleister Guertena. He was one of the lesser-known officers. Spent more time in the labs and in boardrooms than on the street. That was our—my job." A soft sigh. "I was there when he decided to force open the Gate to try and give himself a Keeper's power." Never mind that becoming a Keeper didn't work that way. The link had to be formed at the worst moment in one's life. Reaching the Gates as part of an elaborate plot shot that key element dead in its tracks. "It sounded just like this."

He could hear Kade's scowl. "And you let him?"

"No. I killed him. Him and the other dumbass he roped into his little ritual." Adrian opened his eyes. "Then I started walking and didn't stop till I ended up at the Gates. That's how I was called. Still had the blood on my face when the old woman found me."

A moment of silence. "That sucks."

"Yeah," he agreed. "If we have time, I want to talk to Shion. Aleister looked at the Gates and saw power. She thinks they're the key to saving someone she's lost."

"There's no guarantee you can make her see reason."

"That's fine," Adrian said. "I just want to try."

"Better not be sympathizing," Kade cautioned. "She's still trying to end the world as we know it."

He rolled his eyes. Enough of this. "The second you place one person's life over your community, let alone the world, you've stopped being in the right."

She snorted and stepped past him. "Let's close this sucker and get back to work. We've got about a million little rips to investigate, and I wanna see your friend at some point tonight."

Bold words, but Adrian couldn't beat down the flutter of fear in his stomach as they turned to face the screaming, bleeding hole in the universe. This was worse than the portal under Winfrey Station. At least that hole had formed naturally. Whistler had come through here, which meant the hole was still linked to the Gates. That was the kind of thing that killed Keepers, especially tired ones. If they were rested and their minds sharp, he'd have more confidence. The skin under Kade's eyes was bruised almost black, and Adrian—well, he already knew he was a mess. But they had to try.

Kade raised her arm to her face and left a slash of pink lipstick on her bicep. The colour bled outwards, revealing an extensive sealing spell tattooed into her skin. The flesh around it went greyer. She might have swayed on her feet, but Adrian couldn't afford to dwell on that. He breathed in deeply and sang, countering the sourest notes while she coaxed the rest into harmony. Each note turned to slivers of glass in his throat. The crack in the Gate danced before his eyes.

All that he was poured into the void.

It wasn't enough.

With an awful sense of vertigo, he realized he had to pull back before he lost himself. Without Kade, he wouldn't have been able to. But her power retreated at the same time as his, and they were swept up in each other's wake. This was why Keepers worked in pairs: to save each other when no one else could.

They couldn't seal over the crack in the Gate itself. They could, however, cut off the connection between the two ends of the hole. It snapped like a violin string, leaving them with a nasty tear on this side. Closing that over was a cinch in comparison. Soon, that awful noise was fading away.

The Gate was still cracked. Still leaking. But it was leaking into the space between rather than the industrial district, and that was a triumph. Adrian swayed on his feet, simultaneously exhausted and re-energized as new power flooded in to replace what he'd spent. He felt more tired than he ever had before, but a few steadying breaths later, his magical reserves were functional again.

Kade turned a giddy smile on him. "Well, that was fun!" She rubbed at her arm, smearing the pattern into an indecipherable blur. "Anything else you wanted to cover before we start closing the rest?"

Adrian mostly wanted to go sleep for the next week. But they needed to locate and contain the biggest tears. That would give them a little longer to find where Shion Matreva had hidden herself. Even if the idea of spending the rest of the day on his feet made him want to cry. Adrian let his head fall back, gazing up at the cloud-covered sky. "What do you bet Shion's holed up somewhere right under our noses?"

"No bet. Now come on. I forgot to draw you a map earlier, so we might as well do it at your place."

Their footsteps were quieter than they should be, overlapped and distorted by a million screaming holes in the world.

V

THE RESTRUCTURING WAS underway, but the theory side of the preparation had run into a bit of a snag. Shion had designed this ritual under the assumption that she would have to beat off willing assistants with a stick. In reality, being on the Keepers' watch list had closed many doors before she even began. Gathering twelve practitioners of adequate skill, power, and resolve had been a strain on her limited resources. Janine had been the best of the lot; that was why Shion had relied on her to administrate the ritual. Then Janine had made a judgement call, placing Shion's safety over the ritual's success. She might have saved Shion's life in the process—had certainly saved their workspace from having that thing land in the middle of their delicate arrays—but it had cost them. Now they were down a member, and Shion had no clue where to get a replacement. She'd tweaked her runes and reduced harmonies wherever she could, but there was no use denying it: the minimum number of people she needed was thirteen. Twelve might take them to the Gate but wouldn't be enough to open the blasted thing.

The pen in her hand creaked ominously. She set it down carefully and forced her fingers to unclench. To come so close and then fail…no. There had to be something she could do.

A chirping, high-pitched voice tugged her out of her thoughts. "Shion?"

Her mouth curved automatically, banishing the shadow of rage behind a smile. "Yes, Maria?"

"How much longer will this take?" the girl asked, shifting from foot to foot. "The others are starting to get worried. The Keepers have been poking around."

It took a few seconds for the words to sink in. Then Shion shot to her feet, knocking her chair to the ground in her haste. "They have?"

Maria nodded, anklets jingling as she danced in place.

"Where?" Shion demanded. "When were they seen?"

When they'd first met, Maria had been a bitter little thing, quick to take offence. Now, she was calm enough—and dedicated enough to their cause—to ignore Shion's angry tone and focus on answering the questions. "Downtown. Nobody I talked to was certain about the exact times, but I think the first confirmed sighting was in the morning. Folks have been jumping at shadows all day."

Shion took a breath and forced herself to calm down. She couldn't afford to panic. If the Keepers had already begun investigating, she had no doubt they'd find her hideout within twenty-four hours. Their morals were lacking, but it was difficult to overstate their effectiveness. She had a day to find a way to rework this ritual and save the man she loved. Maybe less.

"Were there any identifying features?" Shion winced the moment the words were out of her mouth. Of course there weren't any identifying features. These were Gatekeepers she was dealing with.

"Somer's been spotted in a few places, popping in and out of existence, picking up after us. His partner's still unknown."

Adrian Somer, male, twenty-six if the files she'd hacked into could be trusted. He lived on Terrace with very little attempt at concealing his presence—had for at least seven years. She'd gone searching for anything that could help her predict his actions and turned up nothing. His paper trail was infuriatingly bland. Someone had gone through a lot of trouble to give him a new start, but there was nothing to hint at why. All she had to go on was the fact that his appearance neatly coincided with the fall of the Guertenas.

He'd had nothing to do with what happened—Shion knew for a fact that the seventeen-year-old Somer had been checked into a hotel room with a senior Keeper while Yves bled out. There'd been a Guertena bug in the room. She'd watched the other Keeper in the grainy video feed, treating young Somer for hypothermia with methods so mundane they made Shion's fingers itch. If Shion had been there at the time, it would have been easy for her to draw the blueness from his lips and ease the shivers wracking his thin frame. She wished viscerally that she'd been at that hotel instead of taking job interviews. If Somer owed her his life, she'd have some leverage over him.

"I see," Shion murmured, eyes unfocused. "How's our progress?"

Maria scuffed one bare foot. "We're basically done. Just waiting on you."

"Ah. I'm sorry, Maria—could you leave me? I need to think."

Being dismissed so abruptly by an adult, even one she trusted, would've sent eleven-year-old Maria into a screeching rage. At fourteen, she dipped her head and marched off, sharp as any toy soldier. The only sign of dissatisfaction were the fists clenched at her sides. Poor thing, Shion thought absently. Maria had been left alone by her father's death, abandoned to an aunt who didn't care for organized magic. She did care for her niece, though. Maria had been forced to sneak out in the dead of night to join the coven, and there'd been a missing-person campaign brewing within the week. So much effort spent winning her trust, convincing her to join and duck the law. Maria would be just as dead as the rest of them if Shion couldn't figure out how to salvage this.

If Janine were still here instead of trapped beyond the Gate, it would be simple. Hell, if Shion had the time to coax one more lost lamb into her flock, it would be simple. Someone who was on the Inside, an above-average magic user scarred by loss. She got up and began to pace. The other Keepers—and there would be at least one more, they never moved alone—were unknown factors. Somer, though…

What did he have? What did he want? How could she arrange this so he could only get it from her?

Shion broke off from her aimless path and headed toward the filing cabinets stacked along the far wall. She'd made printouts of everything that might be useful in case the computers died. They hadn't, but if she spent another second in front of a screen, she might scream. She got down on her knees and rifled through the drawers. Schematics. Diagrams, a fraction of the size required to make their contents functional. A list of backers—those who'd been unwilling to risk their lives but more than willing to fund her. A list of people and organizations that had given her an emphatic "no." A list of dead individuals and disbanded organizations whose resources and infrastructure she could still draw on.

She pulled out the folder on the Guertenas.

Images—mugshots, publicity photos, school pictures—flickered through her vision. Text scrawled under, across, and over them, neat black letters blurring together. She nearly flipped past what she was looking for. It was the flash of familiar hair that made her stop. Pale blond, short in the back, with longer bangs that swept to one side. A style she had seen in photographs and through scrying spells as Somer moved through the streets. The boy on the left side of the snapshot had it brushed right; the boy on the right had it brushed left. Both wore black coats, the broad-collared, hip-length sort that had been in style eight years ago. Shion had owned one too, but she'd lost it—taken it off somewhere and never found it again. The boys in the picture, piercing blue eyes staring out of identical heart-shaped faces, didn't look like the sort to lose things.

The boy on the left was grinning, probably. His teeth were showing, at any rate. His mirror wore a firmly neutral expression, lips pressed into a thin line. They were both terribly young. Too young to have their files in a police database. Too young to have those files marked "deceased."

Shion pulled the folder out and opened it. Leslie and Ashleigh Richter. Twins. Seventeen years old at time of death. A pair of pretty young things one of the Guertena officers had plucked off the streets and molded into monsters. They'd been his bodyguards, assassins, torturers—whatever was necessary, using magic to cover their tracks. The practitioners on the police force hadn't been able to stop them. Lined up, the pieces made for a grim picture: a trail of blood left by two boys barely old enough to drive, while the shadow of the Guertenas kept them safe.

Back then, Shion had been only peripherally aware of how deep the family's roots had sunk into the city; the idea of teenage murderers being allowed to walk free would have been laughable. The world couldn't be that rotten, could it?

It all seemed so obvious now.

She turned the page. Coroner's report. The Richter twins' remains had been dragged out of the private residence of Aleister Guertena. One had been barely recognizable. The other was just ash and fragments of scorched bone, identified by context and proximity. Cause of death for one was a gunshot, point-blank range; the other was too badly damaged to tell. Two things were certain: the fire that consumed the house had been set intentionally and it had been lit after the boys were killed.

The Richters were identical twins. Same haircut, same taste in jackets, same magic—like Shion, they'd been auditory practitioners. Whoever'd written the file hadn't been able to tell which corpse belonged to which brother. They'd had no one to call in; everyone the twins had been close to died or wound up behind bars when the Guertenas went down. An ugly incident with a messy conclusion. When she reached the last page, she felt the writer's relief as the file was closed for good.

She flipped back to the photo. The twins had been caught outside, up against a building—a warehouse, by the looks of it. A straggly little tree peeked over the grinning boy's shoulder. Shion reached out and traced their faces with her finger, adding years and weariness, subtracting neatness. Neither feral grin nor studied calm seemed to fit Adrian Somer. Exhaustion, irritation, a certain harried determination—those worked wonders. Shion sat back, wondering which of them had died and which had walked away. It would be easier to convince him if she knew which name to call.

"It's all right," she murmured. "You can save him. All you need to do is help me reach where they're trapped."

If she could offer the law something it wanted—needed—she would be safe. The Guertenas had taught her that. And unless she was very much mistaken, she could offer "Adrian Somer" everything.

The world was an avalanche of sound scraping on Adrian's nerves. He felt like a bat fluttering through a sea of white noise. Echolocation was a lot less fun in practice. All his senses were working overtime. It didn't take long to hunt down the larger rips—the ones big enough that a small animal or child could stumble through them. Those had to be healed over first. Not all planes adjacent to each other had compatible physics. The smaller holes, just large enough to let through wisps of alien gas, he left for the moment. There were bigger problems to deal with.

Less easy to overlook was the aftermath of yesterday's disasters. Adrian did what he could while still moving and reluctantly left the rest for later, avoiding gawkers like the plague. Even so, he could pick up the shifts in onlookers' signatures as Kade, safely disguised as an anonymous good Samaritan, pushed them off in a safer direction. She had the crowd under control, so Adrian kept walking, listening for the harshest notes in the discordant sea. There seemed to be a pattern to the rips. He couldn't quite nail it down in his head, but they were larger and more numerous around a few specific locations.

The alley he'd found Whistler in was by far the worst.

They didn't find Shion Matreva. Charlie Detlaff and Janine Miller proved similarly elusive. No one had spotted any of the three in several days.

The two of them made it back to his place around seven. Kade walked in silence, her face pinched. All the manic energy she'd shown him that morning had drained away. Not that Adrian was doing any better. He was grateful for the quiet. At least his new wards recognized them both and he didn't need to sing anything to get inside.

Kade stopped on the front step, just inside the protections, and groaned pitifully. Silvery bangs pooled over her eyes.

Adrian pulled the door open and gave her an expectant look. Nothing.

The first time he tried to speak, nothing emerged but a harsh croak. He wet his throat and tried again. Kade remained where she was, listing to the right, still but for the trembling of her hands and the shallow movement of her breathing.

"Coming?" he rasped.

"Yeah," she mumbled. "Just gimme a minute. Tired and gross. I think someone threw beer at me."

"You didn't shield?"

She made a face. "I looked civilian, remember? Katya Yates doesn't know shield spells. And my head hurts."

If he had any skill with healing, he would've offered to help. Instead, he nudged the door open and shooed her inside. She made a beeline for the kitchen, trailing the scent of cheap beer. The sound of pouring water told him she'd turned the tap on, and the hiss that followed said she'd stuck her head under it.

"Feel better now?"

"C-cold!" She reared back, hair flying as she shook her head briskly, then plunged right back in. Water splattered all over the walls. He scowled but kept his mouth shut. Finally, the faucet shut off. Kade wrung out her hair once and flipped it over her shoulder, ignoring the continued dripping. "Thanks. You got paper?"

"Yes. Did you look up Shion's work?"

She pressed her lips together. "Yeah. The details don't match exactly, but the similarities are telling."

"She's had eight years to refine her ritual, but it comes from the same root."

"Great. So it's definitely her." Kade sighed, giving her mass of sopping wet tangles another squeeze. "Show me to your friend?"

"This way."

The living room was quiet. Whistler was still draped across the couch, face down and eerily motionless. Kade paused in the doorway, an odd look on her face.

"What do you see?"

She startled, then shook her head. "I think you're right. I've never seen anything like this outside the Gates. It doesn't seem malevolent or even infectious, but…"

"But he's something that doesn't belong in this world," Adrian finished.

"Yeah. Well, enough stalling! Introduce me to the alien beast. I wanna see the resemblance."

Adrian grimaced. He really should tell her that Whistler probably contained the remnants of Leslie. But that would require telling her about what he'd done to Leslie. He'd rather put that off as long as possible, ideally forever. "He. Not 'it.'"

"Whatever." Kade flapped her hand at the sleeping creature. "Hurry up and wake him."

Whistler hadn't stirred.

Adrian fought down a swell of concern and called out, "Are you awake?"

Awareness. That stolen face tilted up, splitting open in a feline yawn. Rubbery black gums glistened. Slowly, Whistler stretched, digging his claws through the tarp and into the furniture beneath. Something bunched up underneath his thin frame. His legs had finished regenerating. Unlike his arms, which were all but human from the outside, there was no mistaking these limbs for anything but alien. The joints were wrong, a second knee visible, bones lashed together with thick wire. Long, curved blades took the place of toes, and they fidgeted with the same dexterity as the ones on Whistler's hands. All his wounds had closed, leaving dried oil stains. Only a few places still showed the gleam of raw metal: extremities, particularly the digits, tail—tails, now—and back. The awful gouge wasn't quite filled in, but the ruined structure was being restored as Adrian watched. Skeletal wings flexed, arching upward, then settled over frail shoulders.

"What the hell?" Kade whispered.

Adrian elected to ignore her for the moment. "You've been busy."

Mending. Whistler looked past him, eyes bright. *Concern-new. Curiosity.*

"This is my partner, Kade. We're hoping—" The sentence was cut off by a strangled sound. Adrian glanced back and found her doubled over, eyes wide and staring. "Kade?"

She blinked rapidly and raised her hands to her head. "What the hell just happened?"

"Whistler asked why you were here."

"You got *words* out of that?"

Adrian frowned. "You didn't?"

"No! It was—" She yanked at her hair, hissed in pain, and forced herself to stand up slowly. "It was like hearing goddamn Picasso. So many shapes, so many colours, none of them making any sense. I was hearing them, Adrian! You're not supposed to hear colours!"

"Synesthesia?"

"How the hell would I know?" she snapped. "It's just wrong!"

"Don't yell at him," Adrian said sharply. "Whistler—"

Concern, Whistler clicked, coiling back on himself. The bare bones of his wings bristled. *Affront?*

Kade's face turned the colour of tea gone bad. She groaned and clapped her hands over her mouth.

"—maybe stay quiet for a bit," Adrian finished. He wrestled his protective instincts down and helped his partner steady herself.

Whistler watched from the couch, eyes all silver.

"Sorry," she said finally. "I—that was one of the worst things I've ever experienced."

Seemed like unravelling Whistler's speech was harder than Adrian had thought. He wanted to apologize, walk her out, maybe let her drag him to a bar where she could drink away the memory. But Whistler was sitting on the couch, talons curved delicately around a cushion, radiating *concern-curiosity*.

"She's okay," Adrian told him. "Just shaken. Right?"

Kade gave them a wobbly thumbs up. "Yeah. I'll be fine. Give—give me some warning next time. Who knows," she added, picking up steam, "it might make for a neat learning experience. A close encounter of the—oh God it's happening again!"

Confusion, Whistler trilled, reaching up to tug at Adrian's coat. *Postponement. Recollection?*

Adrian grimaced. "Later. Right now, I need you to stop whatever you're doing."

Confusion-uncertainty-sensation. Sensation-mix? Sensation-overlay? Discomfort-sound-image.

It came at him in a barrage of ideas. Adrian scrabbled at them for a moment before he latched onto the unifying theme. "You're communicating through concepts, but that's not how humans are wired usually. We don't have a separate sensory network to pick up magic. Auditory and visual communication is much more common."

Comprehension.

"Magic tends to piggy-back on another sense. I perceive it through sound, which means I can let your intent translate your speech into something I can hear as words." Adrian paused, licking his lips. It was cold out, and they were beginning to crack. "Kade's a visual practitioner. When you open your mouth, she automatically tries to convert what you're saying into images, even though your 'speech' is still being picked up through her ears."

Whistler squeezed his claws together, slicing neatly through the cushion. *Sensory-confusion.*

"Yes," Adrian agreed. That was much simpler and neater than your voice makes her question her sense of reality. "If you could give her a moment to get her bearings—"

"No need," Kade rasped. Her voice was thick and rough, and there was something discomfiting about the way her eyes fixed on the air in front of her. "I'm fine. Just." She made an incomprehensible gesture. "Just get it over with."

Haste-finality? Whistler looked at her, then at Adrian. *Concern. Suggestion.*

"You have an idea?" Adrian echoed.

Confirmation.

He glanced at Kade, who'd begun listing again, to the left this time. "I'm listening."

Whistler sat straight up, bladed tails wrapped around himself. *Sensory-communication. Sensory-overlay. Sensory-communication-intentional. Sensory-overlay-adapt. Negate-discomfort.*

"You think you can communicate with her through visuals?"

Confirmation, Whistler repeated. One tail-tip came to rest on a pale thigh with a faint grinding sound, like a knife being sharpened. *Attempt?*

Kade was blinking rapidly now, her knuckles white at her sides. It was clear she wasn't picking up any of this. Adrian would be surprised if she was even aware of their presence at this point—unfortunate, considering that she was the one who needed to speak with Whistler. For a second, he wondered how it would feel to be in her place.

He closed his eyes and nodded sharply. "Do it."

He didn't have to wonder any longer.

All auditory input ceased. All tactile input ceased. All olfactory input ceased. All gustatory input ceased. Visual input swelled and twisted to compensate in ways he'd never experienced before. The darkness behind his eyes ceased to be. Each breath carried a rush of blue-and-orange-stained purple to his lungs. Muddled browns, greys, and greens lurked beneath his feet in shapes that made his head spin. There was no longer a human shape where Kade had been—just a fractal of white on white on grey. How Whistler appeared was impossible to describe. All around him, there was a sense of movement, but anything he tried to focus on became completely stationary. He was vaguely aware of sitting down suddenly, but that was distant. Unimportant. Pictures flickered in front of him, around him, through him, the thrashing of a mind trying to interpret the uninterpretable.

Things conjured and twisted themselves into being without purpose, operating on dream logic, and like all his dreams, the vision eventually hit something real. The memories pounced, and the whole world sharpened.

He was back in the worst moment of his life.

Rain lashed the windows. Panelled walls swam into focus, their edges loose and transparent. Wood grain danced before his eyes, like a watercolour in progress. The floor was concrete, ridged and layered with countless bumps and grooves. The work of touch practitioners always reminded him of braille, and braille always reminded him of this three-dimensional diagram, this one ritual it was meant to perform. He still had trouble controlling his breathing when he caught a glimpse of braille numbers in the elevator, worse when he accidentally brushed against them. He could see the floor and its diagram in perfect detail, right down to the speckles of crimson at his boots.

He couldn't fight it. Now that this vision had started, he had to see it through. He owed Leslie that much.

The blood grew thicker, less of a spray and more of a swamp. Chunks of unrecognizable viscera were strewn throughout, tiny mountains of flesh and bone rising from the gore. His role in this crime should have been visible. The last crime he had committed as a member of the Guertena family.

A tooth shone white underfoot. Slivers of wet bone gleamed in the fluorescent light. Farther back lay a lock of blond hair, torn from the scalp and stabbed through with a cheap bowie knife. The pattern etched into the blade was anything but simple. It hurt to look at, like sandpaper on the backs of his eyes. This was a spell bound in blood for the simple purpose of causing pain. Attached was a slip of paper, similarly marked, designed to convert that pain into purpose—directing the seething horde of energy contained within the diagram below before the ritual broke. If his other senses were still working, the awful smell of opened entrails would be rippling over him. All that energy had had to go somewhere. Death by backlash. Gruesome, but quick.

Aleister Guertena's demise had barely registered the first time around. Adrian had been too numb to notice it, too lost in his own head to even avoid the mess on his way out. The footprints would have given him away if not for the fire—Aleister's own power leaking out of control, protecting his murderer. Irony. Adrian lingered on the mess, drinking it in not out of guilt or morbid curiosity, but to steel himself against what came next: a cracked, smoking area of flooring where the spray of blood stopped. The centrepiece of this nightmare lay a few metres away, eyes still open, mouth curved upward.

Adrian had almost forgotten that Leslie died smiling.

Once again, he found himself staring down at the small red hole in his twin's forehead. The back of Leslie's skull had shattered, sending brain matter oozing across the floor, but the face was almost intact. Only one small imperfection told the truth.

The final resident of this room—the only one who still lived—stood by the door. Ashleigh Richter was holding a loaded gun, a splash of blood vivid on his cheek, outstretched arm trembling. His eyes were blown wide, fixed on his brother's corpse. He looked terribly young. His mouth was moving. Every couple of seconds, the motion repeated itself. There was no sound, but Adrian didn't need it. He knew exactly what his past self was saying as the first sparks rose from the carvings.

Why? Why did you let him do it?

If he could move, Adrian wouldn't hesitate to bite off his tongue to try and wake up. But he couldn't. He was nothing but eyes locked onto a scene long past.

Why? Why did you let him do it?

What colour would the scream building in his chest be?

Why why why why

"Adrian, can you hear me?"

The world settled back into place as if it had never fallen apart. Adrian's eyes had opened and he hadn't noticed.

A soft trill. *Concern. Health?*

Compartmentalizing this was second nature. Adrian blinked rapidly, banishing the ghosts of his past once again, and forced himself to his feet. "I'm fine," he said, more to himself than either listener. "What happened?"

Kade was sitting cross-legged on the floor. She still looked a bit sickly, but her grin was sharp as ever. "I got to talk to an alien! New species, first contact, hell yeah!"

Whistler let out a loud chirp.

Kade glanced to her left and grinned at something only she could see.

Adrian's head was spinning too much to properly appreciate the byplay. "Congratulations," he said dryly.

"Spoilsport. Your legs gave out like a minute in, so stop trying to act tough and sit down." She patted the floor beside her and turned back to Whistler. "Thanks for sorting things out. Hell if I know how you did it, but I can see what you're saying now. We make it out of this in the same plane of existence, I'm gonna pick your brain. But I should probably introduce myself first, huh? Kade Mauzy, Gatekeeper." For a second, her grin faltered. "Nice to meet you, new coworker."

Identifier-exchange. Greeting. Whistler paused for a moment, then looked at Adrian. *Purpose-self?*

Adrian sat back down. All right, it might've been more of a controlled fall. "Yeah. She's here to try and figure out what you are. Do you know what's going on outside?

Uncertainty.

"Hell," Kade said. "People are dying out there. It's only going to get worse."

"We're trying to stop it. To do that, we need to stop someone else from screwing around with the Gates. We need your help. Especially since you were probably dragged here by the same ritual that's shredding reality to bits right now."

Whistler let out a hum of agreement. *Familiarity. Origin.*

"Thank you." He bowed his head. "I'm sorry you were dragged into this."

Negate-apology. Enthusiasm. A clawed hand reached out and hovered inches from Adrian's cheek. *Familiarity. Recognition. Gratitude.*

A lump formed in his throat as the claws retreated.

"Aw," Kade stage-whispered. "Isn't that sweet? He's happy to have met you. Again, apparently. Speaking of which, I know illusions, and that's no illusion. You wanna explain why the weird metal alien thing has your face, partner?"

There was nothing Adrian would like to do less. But he was out of time. "Yeah. But…gimme a sec."

Hurt? Whistler demanded.

Adrian looked at him, eyes tracing the familiar lines of their shared face. For a moment, he saw a small red hole open in that white forehead.

Concern. Silence. Communication! A clawed hand gestured at him to come closer. *Health?*

"Brain's a little rattled. It's not your fault."

Concern, Whistler clicked. *Confusion. Occurrence?*

"I remembered something." The response was short and clipped, and it made Whistler light up like the sun.

Recollection! Other-familiarity?

That sending had grown far too familiar, and Adrian had run out of excuses to avoid the tangle of concepts within. They flowed over him, into him, relentless and inexorable as the tide. The sheer force of it knocked the breath out of him; a moment later, he was almost glad. Processing the mess felt like drowning in someone else's thoughts.

Being small looking up loud crack a hand in his cool eyes a body that lived a body that died hands that killed a person he would do anything—

Anything—

"I'm sorry." The words dropped like stones from his tongue. "I didn't forget."

Confusion?

Adrian bowed his head. His hair was long enough now to hide most of his face. "I didn't forget," he repeated. "I wanted to. Gods, I wanted to. But I couldn't."

Concern. The flat of a thin blade pressed lightly against his cheek, curved and layered unlike any earthly metal. *Confusion. Clarity?*

"I knew who you were from the beginning. I just didn't want to accept it." The claw went rigid, edges slicing into his face. Adrian laughed shakily. "That's what you've been trying to ask me, right? Who you used to be. Whose memories you're carrying around. Did they show up before or after you got dragged back here?"

An uncomfortable hum rose from Whistler's chest. *After.*

"Thought so." Adrian paused, struggling to line the words up in his head. "Do I seem unfinished to you?"

Observation. Incomplete. Negative-unusual.

"It seems normal to you?"

Affirmative. Whistler's tails began to twist over each other, producing another hideous grinding sound. *Existence-incomplete. Waiting.*

That had all sorts of implications Adrian wasn't going to think about. "I didn't used to be like this. But you already know that."

The silver of Whistler's eyes shrank, leaving only a thin ring. *Confusion?*

"I'm not a twin now, but I used to be one. And unless I'm very much mistaken, you used to be my brother."

VI

Whistler's black stare bored into him like a drill. Adrian could feel the weight of it, but it lacked force. A soft hum built up between them, leaking *confusion* and *familiarity-unfamiliarity-other-familiarity*. Whistler's face was simply blank. Lost. Empty. To the side, Kade let out a long, slow hiss, but said nothing.

Identity-implications? Whistler asked finally.

"It means nothing. Think of it as an echo or a set of old blueprints. Footprints that time has all but wiped away."

Confusion. The next sound out of Whistler's mouth almost made Adrian's heart stop. It was far softer than the version Adrian had made, but the long, drawn-out wail was unmistakable. This was a spell. This was a cry of mourning. This was a name. *Ashleigh?*

He took a shuddering breath and squeezed his eyes shut. Whistler's claws were still cool against his skin; he used their touch to anchor himself. "I used to be. Not anymore."

Confusion. Uncertainty. Identity-loss?

"No." The word came out shakier than he'd like. "It wasn't taken. I just couldn't be that person anymore."

The look in Whistler's alien eyes was all too familiar. *Why?*

"If you were still Leslie, you'd know."

The creature that had been his brother wilted. Whistler shrank into himself, wrapping his shoulders in layer upon layer of steel boning. His wings were still skeletal, but the framework was thicker now. Even his tails fit. It would have been a perfect defence mechanism if the wings had any substance to them. Adrian's cold, dead heart shifted in his chest. He reached out and stroked a slim blade gently.

"It's not a bad thing to forget. I've been wanting to get rid of these memories for—gods, almost a decade now." Adrian shook his head in disbelief. "Was doing fine until yesterday. This isn't going to change anything important. You're still you. Once this is over, I'm still going to try and get you home." Worst-case scenario, he'd put out a request on the WordWeb. The record would probably still be there if he and Kade failed. Maybe whoever or whatever was unfortunate enough to get stuck with their mess would do better.

Lost; Whistler clicked. *Alone.*

"Don't worry. We'll do our best."

Self? Negative. You. Whistler crawled closer. Wireframe wings settled loosely around them both. *Affection.*

Adrian couldn't speak. He couldn't even think. All he could do was stare past Whistler's bony shoulder and seek out Kade's gaze. She made eye contact with him and mimed gagging. The motion stuttered to a halt as she realized he was on the verge of shutting down.

"All right, people," she said, "let's get things moving again. We can sort out our baggage after the day has been saved. Adrian, you got something I can draw a map on?"

Recollection, Whistler whirred in protest. *Knowledge-understanding. Missing-pieces.*

Adrian's breath caught. He couldn't scramble away from Whistler's touch quickly enough. "Butcher paper. Should be in the other room. I need to make a call." He turned on his heel, then paused. "Whistler, when we're done with this, tell us everything you remember of how you were brought through the Gate."

An irritated hum told him Whistler had read Adrian's words as a dismissal. Regret stabbed Adrian's chest, but he kept walking. The entity gazing at his back was many things, but he was not Leslie

Richter. Anything that reached the Gates emerged fundamentally changed. Passing through them? Whistler might have been born from Leslie's death, but he was a new entity. No point in trying to force a dead boy's life and relationships onto someone who happened to share his face. The desire to bring back someone she loved had driven Shion Matreva to become an enemy of reality itself. Adrian refused to make the same mistake.

He'd killed Leslie. He didn't deserve to get his brother back.

The WordWeb's barrier shielded him from Whistler's narrowed eyes.

'identifier?'

He gave it his credentials and rattled off the extension that would take him to the Keepers' emergency message log. "Confirmed Gate access. Confirmed Gate tampering. Something came through. Appears friendly, eats metal, has a loose connection to the local plane of existence and communicates by hijacking perception of magic. Potential new Keeper." He hesitated briefly before continuing. "Potential localized reality failure. If Keeper Mauzy and I are unable to contain it, the effects may spread. Please be ready. And look after Whistler for me."

The silver ocean drained away with the grinding of gears, leaving him a few precious seconds to prepare before facing Whistler again. He opened his eyes to meet a thoroughly judgmental stare. At least Kade had gone, presumably to fetch the paper.

If?

Adrian stared back. "You heard that?"

Affirmative.

So, Whistler could see what happened in the WordWeb's pocket dimension. That was concerning, but they didn't have time to explore the implications.

Adrian steeled himself. "If. This job is as dangerous as my last one. More so, if you count collateral damage."

Death? A short, little burst of static mixed with a tiny, birdlike trill, but somehow there was a world of information packed inside. What, when, how—where? Where. Of course Whistler thought of death as a place. It was where he had been until recently. Beyond the Second Gate.

"Not planning on going anywhere. But yes. It's possible."

A decisive click. FOLLOW.

"No."

Follow. Black eyes glittered mercilessly. *Found. Familiarity. Negative-escape.*

"What, were you looking for me?" Adrian snorted. "You didn't even know I existed until a day ago. We just met and we need each other, so we're working together. Fine. But don't you dare imply that you'd die with me if this failed."

Can you even die again? he did not ask.

Whistler's snort sounded like a tiny car backfiring. *Incorrect. Importance-self-determine. Affection. Death-familiarity.*

"Oh, don't even try. Just because you died once—" His jaw snapped shut at the mutinous expression on Whistler's face. He'd never seen it in the mirror, but it still felt like being punched in the stomach. For seventeen years, that had been Leslie's default state of being. "Stop." Adrian turned away, unwilling to see the effect his words might have. "I'm not going to have this argument with you." He couldn't afford to. "I won't let you die."

The words *not again* went unsaid.

Survive. Teach. Mend.

Adrian wanted to laugh. Whistler had none of Leslie's ability to judge people if he thought Adrian could teach him anything. Still... "I'll do my best."

He could almost hear the creak as plastic lips curved upward. *Acknowledgement. Pleasure. Anticipation.*

Adrian waved a hand, unwilling to make eye contact again. "Kade will be back soon. Sorry in advance if she says anything unfortunate."

Cruelty-intent?

"No, she doesn't mean to hurt you. But it's amazing how much damage you can do by accident." Adrian headed for the kitchen. He needed something to do. "I'll see what I can find for dinner. Let me know if you think of anything. Anything relevant," he amended hastily, as Whistler began to vibrate with an all-too-familiar energy. Leslie had also taken the chance to annoy Adrian whenever Adrian had handed him an opportunity.

Something that felt entirely too much like *spoilsport* brushed past his senses. When not injured or distraught over being misunderstood, Whistler was far too much like his brother had been. That made the differences stand out all the starker.

He hadn't gotten his brother back. He needed to keep that in mind. Otherwise, he'd destroy the fragile life he'd managed to build in the ruins of Leslie's death.

KADE RETURNED A few minutes later with a huge map and extracted a pack of markers from her purse. Adrian abandoned the cupboards he'd been perusing to help her draw. There hadn't been anything but instant noodles and dry bread in there anyway. The map attracted Whistler's interest, which meant explaining what it was meant to do, which meant explaining Shion Matreva. Whistler took the revelation that he'd been dragged through the Gates by a grieving criminal with grace. The worst he did was whistle mournfully when Yves Saunders was brought up.

Kade's description of the damage the summoning had caused was not received as well.

Unnecessary! Pain-collateral-unnecessary! Whistler gnashed his steel teeth.

"I feel you," Kade said. "It sucks and we're gonna stop it." She sighed. "The localized issues we've been having are probably the result of Matreva's spells. If things continue, though, we're gonna see some side-effects of the Gates being tampered with."

Self?

"Like you," she agreed. "I'm assuming the other side is super weird. You look at least semi-human and seem to have a passing familiarity with our world, and we can communicate, so wherever 'there' is can't be that different. It can't be that similar, either, since your biology is totally alien. Assuming 'biology' is the right word. I've been scanning you since I walked in and it's like there's nothing alive in you at all. Your body might look like ours, but the resemblance isn't even skin deep. Seriously—that stuff that looks like skin? It's more like plastic, but not any plastic I'm familiar with." She began speaking faster, staring through Whistler rather than at him. "He's not breathing, his internal circulatory system doesn't seem to serve a purpose except to ferry that oil inside him from one end to the other, and I still can't make heads or tails of how his communications work—"

A long, drawn-out whine. *Uncertainty. Self-invasion?*

"Kade," Adrian said sharply. "He's a person, not a lab rat."

She blinked at him. The lack of understanding was jarring. "It's so cool, though."

"You didn't even ask first."

"Fine." She stared intently at something unseen, then shrugged in Whistler's direction. "Guess I should apologize? I mean, I had to scan you a bit to make sure you weren't dangerous, but yeah. Probably should've asked first before I did any more. My bad."

Uncertainty. Acceptance? A noise that sounded a bit like a car backfiring and felt like a cough. *Discussion-continue.*

"Yay, forgiveness." Kade pumped her arm in tired enthusiasm. "Anyways, it looks like Matreva tried to open the Second Gate and failed. Could've been improperly distributed rune matrices, malfunctioning equipment, magical typos, anything's possible. Point is, when she broke that tiny hole in the fabric of the universe, it had a ripple effect, which is why the whole town is shredding itself to bits right now. Good news is that things haven't gone past the point of no return."

"And the bad news?" Adrian asked.

"The bad news is she's already altered the ritual to make it more resilient than the version we have, and it probably survived the initial failure. If we're lucky, she's given up and gone back into hiding. Are we lucky, Adrian?"

"No."

"Then she's probably gathered her forces and is preparing to make another attempt at opening the Gate. She manages that, and it's the end of the world as we know it. No pressure."

Adrian filed that away with everything else he couldn't afford to think about. "How far along would you say the alterations to the ritual were?"

"Too far. We have one more day, max."

Haste, Whistler chirruped.

"We'll have to act before then." Adrian grimaced. "Time to finish this. Give me your red marker."

Stretched out, the map took up most of the living room floor. Adrian and Kade held it down from either end while Whistler surveyed it from above. After some deliberation, a not-quite-perfect circle was scrawled over the industrial district, with the alley where Whistler had landed marked by a lopsided star. Every major hole in reality was jotted down as an oval of dark blue, avocado green, or hot pink, brightest colours corresponding to the nastiest rips. The points lined up nicely. Too nicely. They might as well have drawn an arrow pointing to a specific neighbourhood between the industrial district and downtown.

Kade made a face. "I don't like how quick that was."

Adrian gazed down at the paper. "Me neither."

Whistler drew his claws together with another knife-sharpening sound. *Inaccuracy-representation.*

"I know it's not the best map ever drawn," she grumbled. "Gimme a break, I've been up for days. I'm running on empty."

"Either it's a trap or Shion is desperate." Adrian jabbed his finger onto the map, tracing a smaller circle around the neighbourhood. "Either way, we have to investigate."

Whistler leaned forward until most of his body was off the couch, sinking his tails into the furniture to keep from overbalancing. *Familiarity-surprise.*

"It's quite close to where you came through."

Agreement. Black eyes flicked up, meeting Adrian's for a moment. *Other-familiarity.*

Adrian took a steadying breath. "Shion Matreva and her group are somewhere in here. What are our options?"

"We could call in an air strike?" Kade suggested. He glared at her until she wilted. "It was a joke."

He leaned forward over the map. "We won't be able to sneak in. So here's what we're going to do."

Both his partners for the operation listened. And when he was done laying out his plan, they gave him identical Cheshire cat grins.

Kade spoke first. "I like it. I'll start drawing up spells. Whistler, focus on healing up and rack your creepy alien brain for anything that might help us. Adrian, either try narrowing down Matreva's location further or talk about whatever's eating you."

"Nothing is eating me."

Falsehood.

Kade nodded approvingly at Whistler. "Think we can get this going in an hour or so?"

Adrian sighed. "Two might be safer."

Agreement.

"Two, then. In the meantime, I'm serious. You two should talk—you've clearly got some baggage to cover. I'll even leave the room." She stood up and winced. "Ah, pins and needles, I hate you so."

Adrian glowered at her for a second, then switched his attention to his monochrome twin. "Do you understand the potential effects of Shion's work?"

Whistler grinned. Death! Destruction! Purpose-other-understanding.

"Glad you have your priorities in order."

A sound that could only be described as a cackle. *Familiarity. Affection.*

Adrian shivered and turned away, following Kade's progress across the room. The blatant eavesdropping was slowing her down. "Fine, we can talk. Let's eat first."

She made a face and left quickly. Adrian didn't know what she was making so much fuss about. It wasn't like he was planning to make her cook.

Wait, she'd been alone in the kitchen for a while. She knew his cupboards were empty. That explained it.

Whistler was finally well enough to leave the couch, so Adrian got a front-row seat to watching him try and figure out chairs. Double knees and twenty-centimetre-long bladed digits did not mesh well with standard-issue furniture. He finally settled for crouching sideways on the seat and propping his claws up on the table, facing forward in a feat of inhuman flexibility. Dinner was toast for Adrian and tinfoil for Whistler, who complained about the taste and then ate the entire roll. Adrian shook his head and made a mental note to pick up something more filling whenever he next had time to drop into a hardware store. Nails, perhaps. Or lead piping. He'd ask Whistler for ideas.

But by the end of the day, Whistler would be safely back behind the Gate, so there was no point in making plans.

Hurt? Whistler snapped up the last scraps of shiny metal and gave him a recognizably concerned look.

"No, just thinking. You?"

Whistler scrunched up his face in disgust. The odd skin of his face didn't crease right, but the sentiment was visible. *Confusion. Unclear.*

"Having trouble remembering?"

Negative. Fast. Open-tear. Fall.

"That's it?" Adrian asked. "You just fell through the crack?"

Whistler's head jerked in one of his mechanical nods. *Fall. Hurt.*

Injury-landing.

"Were you hurt before or after you landed?"

Before. Claws drummed softly on an armrest. *Tear-shut.*

That couldn't be right. If Shion Matreva's ritual had been what cracked the Gate—and Adrian couldn't think of anything else that might have done so—Whistler would have been drawn through the hole, sure, but it couldn't have shut on him before he was all the way through. Not without seriously damaging Shion's base of operations. That much Gate energy would poison the surrounding area for weeks without a Keeper to deal with it. If the infected wound Kade described had been opened in the heart of Shion's spellwork, the whole thing would've rotted from the inside out. But Whistler had come through in an alleyway, not Shion's workshop, and the oozing portal was blocks away from any fragile workings. That wasn't the kind of work Adrian expected of—well, anyone but another Keeper. Redirecting an interdimensional portal on the fly was hard even when you were made to manage such things. Non-Keepers could make up for lack of power with enough preparation, but if Whistler's story was correct, whoever'd changed the portal's end point had had none.

That meant… "We're looking for a body."

Confusion.

"We assumed that you were set down where the caster intended you to be. Otherwise, they'd have had to alter the spell and change the destination of the portal in a few seconds while you were coming through. That's not something an ordinary practitioner can do without some serious back-up. Someone to draw power from. Someone whose perceptions are clearer and can be used as a filter." Adrian gave Whistler a measuring look. "If they'd used you to guide the spell and do the heavy lifting, I could buy it—you speak magic, you hear magic, you are magic."

A steady mechanical purr. *Flattery.*

"You're putting yourself back together as we speak."

Still.

"The point is that there's a limited number of people who could do something like that. You didn't, obviously, because you were the one being redirected. A rogue Keeper could do it, but not without being detected. A particularly gifted practitioner might be able to do it once, but they'd burn themselves out. Too much power."

Confusion. Implications.

"They'd die," Adrian said grimly. "There's a huge difference in power between someone who studies magic and someone who is magic."

Whistler cocked his head to the side. *You?*

"The latter. For better or worse. Kade, too—all Keepers are. It's why we can do what we do—and why we need to do it in the first place."

A pensive click. *Purpose.*

Adrian smiled. Technically. Lips were pulled up and teeth were shown, at any rate. "Yeah. The Gates feed us their power. In turn, we do our best to keep people safe—from them, from magic, and in general. We became a formal organization so we could be as honest as possible without putting everyone in danger. Sometimes, that means dealing with the magical equivalent of natural disasters—stuff nobody can prevent—but mostly it means cleaning up other peoples' messes so they don't end up dead or worse. That's a part of saving the world, too."

The First Gate had always been open, but there were countless spells scrawled and carved and burnt at its foot. Spells that had been placed there before any written or oral history began, when the fossil record implied that humanity was still in the alpha stages of development. Spells that made no sense to anyone who lacked a Keeper's innate understanding of all things related to the Gates; the pieces that had been made public were viewed by most practitioners as useless and probably fake. A whole system of magic, and all memories associated with it, lost. Who had left them no longer mattered.

Those people were gone—wiped away as if they had never existed. Opening the First Gate had been the end of the world, an end so thorough that no one even knew what had changed.

Had sound been trapped behind spiderweb and silver leaf? Language? Thought? There was no way to know. Whatever it was, it had already been unleashed.

It was the Second Gate they had to worry about now.

Adrian's gaze was drawn back to Whistler. His inverted image, a third doppelganger to Ashleigh and Leslie Richter, two boys who were both equally dead. Dead white skin, rubbery flesh stretched tight over a steel framework too thin and spindly to be human. Even his anatomy had shifted; Leslie had transitioned alongside Ashleigh, but Whistler was nearly sexless and barely seemed to understand what gender was. Would Shion be satisfied if her dead lover returned like that? Would she be able to embrace someone whose hands would cut her? Be able to transfer her love to someone whose only knowledge of her came from fragments of another life, who in perfect ignorance trampled on the most important, intimate things about her beloved? Adrian couldn't. That would be the ultimate insult to the brother he'd killed and to whatever Whistler was now.

"If someone is already dead, Shion will be desperate. If that person died because they were trying to save the rest of the coven from some sort of monster from beyond the Gate…" He nodded to Whistler. "Then the survivors will be trying to live up to that sacrifice."

Death?

"They'll probably try and bring whoever it was back. I know Shion's type." If things had gone differently, he might have turned out the same as her. "She'll claim she's violating the natural order for everyone's sake—that way, she can pretend her motives aren't completely selfish even when people are dying around her. More important is the body."

A questioning trill.

"That person died at the actual site of the ritual. Worst-case scenario, the coven dumped the body somewhere nearby, possibly in several pieces. The area we need to search is dramatically reduced, and we pin them with murder or manslaughter charges. Best-case scenario, the corpse is still in Shion's lair. We find it, we find her."

Probability?

"Don't know," Adrian admitted. "But I know how to start looking. Do you remember what it felt like to pass through the hole?"

Affirmative.

"Can you show me? Like you showed things to Kade?"

As it turned out, Whistler could.

Silence. A complete absence of sound. Blindness. Eyes staring into not darkness, but nothingness. Suspension. No texture against skin, bone, supports.

Helplessness. Inability to change direction.

Falling.

Sensation. A light. Many lights, all artificial. Recycled power pouring through crude channels. Others. Unknown selves, shrouded in a haze of strange thoughts. Surrounding the hole through which somewhere could be glimpsed.

Falling. Twisting around as texture returned, unfamiliar gases pressing in from above. Preparation. Landing imminent. Other. Singing loudly into the void, just under-in-front-before the hole in the nothing.

Recollection. Alien. Familiarity-unfamiliarity-other. Uncertainty. Hesitation.

Falling.

Pain!

Adrian came back to himself in stages. Nerves, freshly freed from outside influence, worked overtime as they struggled to restore order. His throat was raw and aching. Had he been screaming? Damn, that was embarrassing. He closed his jaw and swallowed experimentally. The pain was a dull echo of what Whistler had shown him. His eyes had closed at some point. He blinked and immediately screwed them shut again. Whistler's senses were still mingled with his own. Thoughts had a colour. They left stains. Was this how Kade saw the world? If so, he no longer envied her. The couch dripped with weariness and pain, some of it fresh and alien, most old and crusted over. Streaks of grief ran over the windows. Denial and determination blended together, forming a trail to the front door. Depression, hysteria, and something cold, grim, and nameless lurked in the corners.

The residue of a life. His life. Everything he'd been trying to avoid made visible. Leslie's dead eyes stared blindly at him from every surface. He felt sick to his stomach.

Concern. Hurt?

"Fine. Gimme a minute." He'd gotten what he wanted, at least. Somewhere in the jumble of inhuman memories rattling around his head was the moment of disruption—the moment when things had gone from bad to worse. The burst of agony had drowned out most of it the first time he experienced Whistler's memories, but as he replayed the sensations, he was able to pick them apart. Beneath the phantom ache of severed limbs lay awareness of where the ritual was intended to bring Whistler, and more importantly, those who'd opened the way for him.

Thirteen. And then, after the burst of pain, twelve. Shion had been traditional. Sensible, even. Numbers had power, and she must have needed every scrap she could accumulate to pull off her plan.

She'd need a replacement now.

If the worst came to pass, he'd follow Kade's half-joking suggestion and rain fire down on Shion's head. No one life was worth trading the continent of North America for. Full scorched-earth tactics would eliminate the ritual, regardless of casualties. Then Adrian would leave the city and go on indefinite suspension. Someone would review his case and decide whether he'd made the right choices. Whether it was worth putting him back on duty or if he needed to be retrained from the ground up. He'd been a murderer to begin with. That left him on thin ice. There were a limited number of Keepers, but that didn't mean they were never made to retire. But if he was reading things right, there was no need for things to go that far.

"Whistler, you tore the ritual apart when you came through. If we plugged you back into the spellwork, do you think you could do that again?"

Affirmative.

That sounded way too close. He screwed his eyes open as far as he dared and groaned. "Whistler, get off the table."

Negative. Concern.

Adrian decided not to argue. They had an actual win condition now. All they had to do was hook Whistler into the heart of the ritual and let his presence unravel it. Adrian wouldn't be able to do it, but Whistler was different. No one knew more about the Second Gate than he did.

First, though, the body. The signature of the dead practitioner was fresh in Adrian's memory. She'd been young and an avid spellcaster. The type who, having learned that magic was real, insisted on using it for everything, but she'd had the power to back it up. A gifted independent with an outlook that invited more experienced practitioners to take advantage. Shion must've been overjoyed to find her. When he closed his eyes to concentrate, the bright glow of fear, worry, and *bonds* lit up the inside of his eyelids. Janine Miller had loved her coven fiercely and without hesitation. When the time had come to choose between her life and the goal they'd dedicated themselves to reaching, she'd sacrificed herself willingly.

Anger, Whistler hummed. *Why?*

"It's nothing."

A reproving click. *Lying. Explanation.*

"The woman who died sacrificed herself without telling the person—people—she was doing it for."

Anger? Whistler repeated with a different emphasis.

"I don't appreciate that sort of mindset," Adrian said stiffly. "Self-sacrifice can be a noble thing, but if you keep quiet about it, it's too easy for things to go wrong."

Pale lips curved downward. *Familiarity?*

Adrian stood up and turned away from the table. "I don't know. Now come on. We need to make some arrangements."

Whistler shambled grumpily after him as he headed for the hallway and called Kade's name. She teleported in about thirty seconds after he called, appearing in the moment between one breath and the next. She materialized by the butcher paper map, wild-eyed, exhausted, and covered in hand-drawn sharpie butterflies. "Don't judge me" was the first thing that came out of her mouth. "It's a convenient shape to stash spells in."

Adrian pointedly said nothing.

"Shut up and give me the signature."

He reached for the pattern of Janine in Whistler's scattered memories, gathered the notes, and sang them for her. She squinted, looking rather than listening, and for once he didn't have to wonder what she saw. The ghost-like figure of a dead girl hung in the air before them.

"Yeah," Kade said finally. "That'll be Janine Miller."

"You knew her?"

"We crossed paths a few times. Our civilian selves ran in different circles. Besides, I've memorized her face over the last couple days." She glanced quickly at Whistler, then turned back to Adrian. "Can you hear her?"

Adrian nodded.

"Then what are we standing around for?" She flapped her hands, breaking out in a tired grin. "I'll do the illusions. You two, move, move!"

Whistler chirruped and hopped off the chair in a controlled tumble. *Haste!*

Silvery metal flexed, exposed and somehow raw. Adrian hated to puncture their bubbles, but there was something that needed to be addressed before they could go anywhere. "First, you need clothes."

Confusion.

Kade looked at him for a moment, then shrugged. "You do stick out. Got anything he can borrow, Adrian? Don't think he'd fit my stuff."

"And you think he'd be able to wear mine? The joints are all wrong and there's no way a shirt is going to get over those wings."

Suggestion. Covering-requirement-unnecessary.

"Yeah, no. Clothing is mandatory outside the home."

Whistler's eyes flashed silver. *Home?*

"Yes," Adrian said, focusing on the most apparent of the concepts enclosed in that sound and ignoring the rest. Leslie had also been the type who made a point to make himself at home. He couldn't let Whistler do the same thing. "Different rules for different places. We're going out in public, even if the public probably won't notice. It's important to dress the part." And, you know, dress. Period. Magic could work wonders when it came to passing, but clothes were still necessary underneath. Part of the social contract that Whistler needed to familiarize himself with.

Confusion-acknowledgement, Whistler grumbled. *Strangeness.*

"Society has a lot of strange rules and conventions. It's generally agreed to be worth the hassle, though. The price of not being alone."

Those eyes went entirely silver. *Self?*

"Yeah, you too, as long as you're here and willing to play along."

Another searching glance, as if all the mysteries of the universe could be found on Adrian's face. Adrian was suddenly certain that he'd slipped up. Then Whistler blinked, irises shrinking to a more manageable size, and gave them a firm, mechanical nod.

Covering, he chirped, and began to trill.

It was a spell in a format Adrian had never encountered before, sight and weight and texture wrapped in sound. As they watched, a thin layer of slick black spread across Whistler's skin, dripping like oil, running down pale limbs, halting just before wrist and ankle stopped and steel began. Nothing splashed onto the floor. The black substance clung to his body like a second skin, but it covered everything important, even if it looked closer to plastic than cloth. His back was left bare down to the tails, leaving his still-healing wings free, and most of his chest was visible. White flesh and silver muscle peeked through a thousand small holes on each limb, like stars in the night sky.

Whistler grinned up at them. *Better?*

"Better," Adrian agreed.

Kade whistled in approval. "That was nice. You end up sticking around, I'm totally gonna commission you."

Confusion.

"We'll explain later." Adrian headed for the door, grabbing his jacket as an afterthought. "You up for a walk?"

Affirmative. Whistler stretched fluidly and flowed upright. There was something off about his balance—probably had something to do with the way he stood on the balls of his feet—but he was standing.

Kade clapped and stepped forward, holding up a blue marker. "Illusion time. Hold still."

It was only good sense to put on their perception filters before the battle started, and in a form that wouldn't require them to split their attention, but clearly the other side of the Gate did not have a concept of face-painting. Whistler looked hilariously awkward as he struggled not to squirm away. Adrian had no grounds for snickering. This was a serious situation. Besides, it was his turn next.

VII

Adrian didn't quite tear the fabric of local reality searching for his target, but it was a close thing. Janine had been dead long enough that the remnants of her presence were dissipating. Soon only the echo would remain, one more shade to haunt the graveyards. Her song was a happy one, full of string instruments and hope. It wobbled in and out of focus, forcing his full concentration. The bleed-over of Whistler's senses was fading, but Adrian already had her signature.

Kade's perception filter took the form of serpentine scribbles across Whistler's right cheek and Adrian's left. It ensured nobody looked twice at either of them. Whistler remained close, inverted eyes peering at their surroundings with curiosity, becoming steadily more agitated as the song led them into the industrial district. Darkness had already fallen, and the streetlights were flickering on. When they passed the alley where Adrian had found him, Whistler dropped to all fours, arched his back, and hissed.

Based on the current location of Janine's corpse, Shion's group had been holed up in an abandoned warehouse barely two blocks away from the alley. So much for it being a peaceful neighbourhood. She'd known her enemy well enough to block off every trickle of power outside the building. He might have been able to spot the artificial nature of the calm spot if he'd spent a dedicated month examining it from every angle, but he'd never bothered. There was always something more urgent or rewarding to do.

Funny. They'd expected the neighbourhood's peace to be interrupted by something awful. Instead, that peace had been a symptom of something awful.

Kade sighed. "I don't know what's worse—that she got her inspiration from a horror movie or that we didn't notice. She must've been holed up in here for years."

"Don't rub it in." Adrian let his grasp on Janine's signature fade and prowled forward, keeping at least a foot away from the white line of paint screaming "alarm system" at him. Literally. It was too well-made to betray any more details, but it didn't take a genius to figure out the phantom shrieking would turn very real the moment someone crossed the line. "Think you can take care of the perimeter?"

"Who do you think I am?" She crouched to examine the spray paint. Her fingers glowed a soft blue-green.

In seconds, Adrian's head was clear again. He gave the building a measuring look. "Anything else?"

Barriers. Whistler tucked his tails against his back and pressed his cheek against the paint, folding his spine in ways that would have made a contortionist weep. *Death.*

Adrian was grateful he wasn't an olfactory practitioner. If he were, he could probably smell Janine's corpse from here. "The body will be inside, along with Shion Matreva and at least eleven others."

Confirmation.

"Definitely eleven others."

Whistler preened.

Kade chuckled. Then the mirth fled from her face. "No time to break in quietly. Ready for a dramatic entrance?"

Agreement. Begin?

Adrian nodded and took a step forward.

Kade stayed where she was. Her voice was steady as she began counting down. "Three."

A familiar song took shape in his mind.

"Two."

Note by piercing minor-key note, it assembled—a burst of raw hurt and anger and *lashing out.*

"One."

A song that came as easily as breathing.

"Zero."

Adrian didn't categorize all his spells; that rigid approach to magic had never appealed to him. Some spells, though…some spells, he couldn't help but name. Ashleigh's Scream was one of them. The sound that left his throat was a physical thing, blood in his mouth and broken glass on his tongue. The air in front of the warehouse rippled as the barriers shredded, but the Scream didn't stop there. Splinters flew as the walls tore open. Adrian was faintly aware of a screech of alarm and a white light, but it felt distant and unimportant compared to the grief flooding his heart. This happened every time he cast this spell. It never got any easier.

Leslie was dead. Leslie had been dead for almost a decade. Ashleigh had killed him. He'd watched the life flee his brother's eyes and he hadn't been able to say a damn thing but "why?" Ashleigh's Scream was everything the man who'd become Adrian Somer had never been able to say, every sob, plea, and threat honed into a burst of raw, auditory destruction that ripped apart anything and everything in its path.

The warehouse stood no chance.

Shion and Adrian had one thing in common: they'd both poured all their grief into a spell. But Ashleigh's Scream wasn't a rejection of loss, just an expression of it. The Scream wasn't even a particularly dangerous spell—it passed harmlessly through living matter. Its only purpose was to tear down the walls that stood in his way at the cost of reliving the worst moment of his life.

The air in front of them rippled again as the spell rebounded, turning back toward Adrian. He let the last of his air puff out and closed his eyes, waiting for the memory of cold rain on his skin.

Rejection!

Adrian looked up just in time to see a flash of silver and black throw itself in front of him. Whistler shrieked, an electric sound that ate up every other noise around it. Flickers of affection and hurt battered at Adrian's thoughts, pushing away the numbness of that rainy day. The Scream crashed into Whistler's spell and stopped. Wings flared out around them. The outer plates were growing back in, shaped like long, skinny arrowheads. Almost like feathers.

Concern. The clicks rang out like gunshots. *Adrian?*

Adrian smiled. "Stop worrying about me, idiot."

Whistler huffed. *Ingrate.*

It was Kade's turn. She stalked forward, arms glowing to the elbow, mouth curved in a fiendish grin. Her shadow was huge, cloaked, and menacing, but she was intimidating enough without the illusion.

The warehouse's outer wall was entirely gone, and its absence was having a negative effect on the building's overall stability. That it hadn't collapsed said more about the skill of Shion's coven than that of the architect. Lucky for them, the Scream's range had been too short to hit the opposite wall; Adrian doubted the building would have survived that. Eleven figures stood in a loose circle at the edges of a sprawling spell diagram. The largest was a heavyset man in his late forties, the smallest a waif-like teenage girl. All of them were frozen, wearing identical expressions of shock. In the centre, Shion Matreva floated a foot off the ground, eyes closed. She looked peaceful. Like she hadn't even registered their arrival.

One of Kade's butterfly drawings shattered on her skin. When she spoke, her voice was almost unrecognizable as human. "By order of the Gatekeepers, I'm taking you into custody! Everyone on the ground, now!"

There was a split-second delay between her words and the coven's reaction. By then she'd halved the distance between them, and her first spell was taking effect. Adrian saw the sudden pallor on their faces, the way they trembled, and shivered in sympathy. Fear and guilt auras were never pleasant. Add in the deep-rooted knowledge they'd done something wrong, and you had yourself a recipe for immediate, non-violent surrender. He wasn't surprised when most of them fell down and cowered. He sang a quick barrier to keep the surrendering practitioners in one place and safe. Only two stayed on their feet and dodged his spell: the big man and the little girl. Both of them were already building spells of their own. They cast almost simultaneously. Adrian countered with softer notes as he and Whistler slipped inside. The shield he'd been weaving snapped into place around Kade just in time. The man looked around wildly, searching for him, but the girl regained control of herself more quickly.

"Charlie, focus!" she yelled, small fingers tracing patterns in the air. A tactile practitioner, then. Her partner was visual, judging by the glow surrounding his hands. Neither needed reagents or materials for their magic.

That would be an advantage if they weren't facing Keepers.

Brown foundation dripped down Kade's arms, revealing a set of elaborate, shifting tattoos. They shone iridescent. When Adrian looked at them, he heard a soft hum, the sound almost drowned out by the rising crash of their opponents' next move. A bell rang out as the girl began dancing in a specific pattern. After a second, he recognized the intent behind those movements: a binding. She wasn't trying to fight them, just restrict their movement long enough for Shion to finish. Brave, but—

Adrian threw himself to the side, narrowly avoiding a burst of heat aimed at his chest. The man had clearly found his focus.

The girl took advantage of Adrian's momentary distraction to finish her spell. With a sharp *crack*, the floor split open, sending a cloud of dust soaring up. Both remaining foes were on the other side. So was Kade. Whistler was on his side, and he didn't know how to feel about that. If it were Leslie, he'd need to watch his back from his own ally. His brother would never forgive him for what he'd done. But it wasn't Leslie who sat up on his haunches, shaking the dust from slick black hair and blinking inverted eyes. There was no malice in that gaze. Only expectation and something Adrian was determined to interpret as concern. He hummed a communication spell into being and rolled smoothly to his feet.

"Can you handle them?"

"I have these two," Kade said. "Deal with Matreva."

He broke the connection as Whistler darted up on all fours, eyes wide and silver. *Attention!*

The subtly discordant symphony was building to a crescendo. This time, it took him a second too long to put the pieces together. When he turned, Shion's eyes were open. She was looking directly at him.

All things considered, Shion Matreva was not an intimidating woman. She looked older than her thirty years, her round face sallow from lack of sunlight, and she had almost a decade's worth of baggage under her eyes. Her clothes were stained and wrinkled, her curly hair a nest of snarls. Chalk dust clung to her socks and pen stained her fingers. She swayed slightly with the effort of staying in midair, but the smile she turned on him was warm.

"Mr. Richter," she said, "how nice of you to make it."

The words on his tongue turned to ash. How—?

"Confused?" Her smile widened. "It wasn't that hard to figure out the connection between Adrian Somer and the Richter twins. You didn't even bother to change your face. I suppose you were counting on the stress to age you quickly. Didn't quite work, I'm afraid, though you do look a fright."

A soft metallic sound came from behind her. *Help?*

Adrian found his voice in time to growl a negative and refocus on her. The ritual was in motion, but it wasn't ready yet. "Hello, Ms. Matreva. Or would you prefer Shion?"

"That depends on why you're here. I prefer to be on first-name basis with my friends."

So that was how this was going to go. "Think about what you're doing, Ms. Matreva. It's not too late to stop this. No one else needs to get hurt tonight."

"No one needs to get hurt at all," she said. "That's why I need to do this. Why *we* need to do this."

"People have already died." His voice grew hard despite himself. "Can't you hear the city screaming? You need to stop before this gets worse."

Her mouth twisted. "It's fine. They'll come back. As soon as I have proof of concept, the whole world will be beating a path to my door."

"That's…not going to happen." Did she really think she'd be lauded for shutting down a metropolis? The casualties were still being counted, practitioners and ordinary people alike. He exhaled slowly, trying to keep calm. "Break the spell. I'll take the backlash. Then we can talk this out." As long as she hadn't already breached the Gates, he wouldn't be in serious danger. The backlash wouldn't be nearly strong enough to burst holes in his brain, let alone tear his body apart like it had Aleister's. He could bear it.

"It will," she said with utter certainty. "You came here for a reason. From the moment you heard about this spell, you couldn't stop thinking about it, could you?" Her voice was velvet, worming its way into his ear like a nest of spiders. "You tried. Oh, Lord, did you try. But all you could do was bury it under layers of moralizing and duty. And underneath, you were always thinking about the one you'd do anything to see one more time."

Distress? Concern.

Adrian clenched his fists, nails biting into the flesh of his palms. He didn't dare make a sound for risk of drawing Shion's attention to Whistler. How she'd missed him, Adrian didn't know—maybe she'd mistaken Whistler's alien signature for an extension of Adrian's own Gate-fuelled power. Maybe the two of them still sounded similar enough for Whistler's cries to be lost in Adrian's steadier presence. Didn't matter. As long as she focused on him, Whistler could crack the ritual with impunity. He needed to keep her attention.

Even if it meant listening to this.

"How did you feel when you learned your brother had died?"

"I didn't," he bit out. He'd been the one to kill Leslie. He hadn't deserved to feel.

She nodded. "It didn't feel real. You thought there must have been some mistake—that this message was meant for someone else. You kept feeling that way, until you saw the body."

Wrong on every count. Leslie's death had been the only real thing. The weight of it had crushed him. The sound of rain had swallowed everything else.

"You wanted to change things. To reject that impossible truth. Well, here's your chance—" A pause. Brief, but unmistakable. "Leslie."

Wrong again. Adrian closed his eyes and breathed out slowly. When he looked up, he could feel the same certainty in her voice settling over his shoulders. "My name is Adrian Somer. Your stronghold has been uncovered and partially demolished. Your allies have already surrendered or been apprehended. You've lost. Stop the ritual. I don't want to hurt you, Ms. Matreva, but the second you decided Yves Saunders was worth the lives of everyone in this city, dealing with you became my responsibility."

All at once, the warmth vanished from her face. "At least I didn't give up on Yves! Have you thought about your brother once since he died? He was your other half! How could you say you loved him if you let him slip away?"

Ha. How could he, indeed?

If only he hadn't loved his brother. Then looking at Whistler wouldn't hurt so much.

Progression. Attention-hold. Soon. Adrian was dimly aware of Whistler pacing around the edge of the diagram, humming quietly as he digested its components. Everything else was put into holding back the blazing heat Shion's words had ignited.

When he finally spoke, it was soft and terribly quiet. "Everyone's lost someone, Ms. Matreva. There's nothing wrong with wanting them to return. But you've traded hundreds of lives for Yves's already.

Do you really think you can just undo that?"

"Yes! That's what magic is for!" The ferocity of her response seemed to surprise her. "That's what it's for…erasing our mistakes."

"That's not how life works. Actions have consequences. You can't snap your fingers and expect to fix everything."

"But we can. We have the power." She smiled bitterly. "You've lost someone. We all have. We hurt and we scream and we beg, but nothing changes, so we learn to live with that pain. But Adrian, we don't have to do that anymore."

Adrian could see how she'd gathered allies so quickly. To the inexperienced practitioners she'd approached, her intensity must have been irresistible. It was enough to catch him off guard; they must have been drawn to her like moths to a flame. For a moment, he wanted nothing more than to see that fire rise higher and higher—to warm himself by her fervor. To stop blaming himself for things he couldn't have changed and start blaming the world. To see Leslie again, no strings attached, and think of his brother without the crushing weight of guilt. He'd take back his old name, his old self, and all the stains and discomfort that came with them as long as it meant having his brother back.

But she wasn't the only one who'd lost everything. Just the only one who burned.

"There's so much death in the world. So much suffering. Reducing it, even a little, is a worthwhile endeavour." Her eyes stared beseechingly into his. "The Keepers thought I was going to overturn society, but that was never my intention. All I want is to bring back the people we've lost."

Overturn society? Ha. If that was all she'd intended, Adrian would stand back and let her. He suspected Kade would, too. But the woman who was willing to throw away the world for love wouldn't be content with simply changing it.

Around them, the noise rose to a fever pitch. "Even if you bring Yves Saunders back, he won't be the same. The Gates always leave their mark. What will you do if he returns with the body of a demon? If he doesn't remember you?"

"I'll fix him."

"You'd really sacrifice the world to save one person?"

"Don't you dare pass judgement on me," she hissed. "You'd do the same if you had the chance."

Wrong, wrong, wrong, wrong. "Don't lump me in with you!" he snapped.

Despite everything, Shion Matreva smiled. "I don't have to. Your power's been leaking out for the last ten minutes, worming its way into my ritual. You can pay lip service to the Keepers all you want, but you gave me what I needed to save him. Save them." A tired but radiant smile. "Thank you. You chose love after all."

Whistler jerked like he'd been exposed to an electric current and pulled back, leaving only one clawed finger touching the diagram. *Success!*

Adrian laughed, a broken, ragged sound. So Whistler's magical signature really was indistinguishable from his own. That meant it was also indistinguishable from Leslie's.

Matreva really was a fool. There was no fixing what his brother had become. And even if there were…it would destroy Whistler as surely as Leslie had been destroyed. As surely as becoming Ashleigh Richter again would destroy Adrian.

"No. Between love and the world, I always chose the world."

Her eyes had just enough time to widen before the spell roared to life and everything crumbled away.

THE PLACE BETWEEN places was, in some ways, very similar to Whistler's sensory-overwrite, only worse. The human brain wasn't meant to process nothingness. It could learn and it could endure, but there would always be a bone-deep wrongness, an inborn understanding that this wasn't something people were meant to experience.

When it came to dealing with that which one was not meant to know, any protection was invaluable. Even the fragile skin of one's eyelids was a shield against the emptiness.

There was no warning now. No protection. No time for any of them to brace themselves. Just the absence of light, of sound, of anything. They hung in limbo. The ritual symphony screeched to a halt, and a familiar whisper flooded in to replace it.

Ashleigh. Ashleigh.

"Ashleigh!"

It was uncomfortably warm in the basement. The air was thick like molasses. Someone had been playing with the worst kind of magic, and this heat was a side effect. Leslie was on the other side of the room, bleeding. He was still on his feet, but that wouldn't last long. The lines of pain were clear on his face even as he broke into a grin.

"Followed me, didn't you?" Leslie accused playfully, clutching at his upper arm. Blood dripped steadily from between his fingers. "Shouldn't have done that."

"What is this?"

"What is what?" Leslie's laugh was always rough and grating, but now it sounded like breaking glass. "Don't play dumb, brat. You know this is exactly what it looks like."

That was a cue for him to hiss that he was only a few minutes younger, to defuse this situation and turn it into something other than what it was. A cue he couldn't take. Not with the end of the world screaming in his ears. His grip on the gun tightened. "How long?"

Leslie stopped laughing. "Al's been planning this for years."

He shook his head, reaching for the comforting certainty of denial. "This is suicide."

"No," said someone on the far side of the room. "It's the final step in our business plan."

He had his weapon up and trained on the speaker before he recognized his employer.

"Destroying the world?" he asked incredulously.

"Don't be overdramatic," Aleister Guertena admonished. "There will still be a world after this. A better one."

He backed up a step, keeping the gun steady in his hand. "There won't."

Couldn't they hear it? The sound of reality slowly shredding under the weight of endless grave dirt, old bones, and rusting metal? Didn't they know what would happen if the future implied by that awful noise came to fruition?

"Ash. Bro. Idiot. It's okay." Leslie groaned, accompanied by the sound of liquid dripping to the floor. "It's only a door. Doors are meant to be opened. All the hard work's already done. One little ritual left, and we're all good. No more killing. Unless we want to," he added quickly, too late to cover the slip.

"You want out." The words dug into his tongue like knives. "You want out so bad *this* seemed reasonable."

He shouldn't have been talking. Aleister was a good practitioner—much more experienced than either twin. But Aleister was wreathed in a tangled web of power so complex and delicate that the slightest twitch would cause it to cave in. Spell backlash was an ugly way to die. They'd been too thorough at removing anything that might interfere, up to and including the weapons both men habitually carried. There was the knife, but the knife was part of the ritual—stabbed through a lock of Leslie's hair, wet with Leslie's blood. Only one lethal weapon left in this room.

"Put the gun down, son."

He kept it trained on the man who'd taken them in off the streets. The ridges on the floor bucked against his feet, screaming through his bones louder than any spell he'd heard before. If it were a real sound, he'd have been deafened. So much power. So much potential. All spent reaching for somewhere—something—that should not be touched. How could they stand the helpless keening of reality as it was ripped asunder?

Aleister smiled, his aura of triumph unwavering even with a gun in his face. Clearly the tortured screams meant nothing to him. Leslie, though—Leslie was shuddering now, barely upright until he realized who was looking at him. Then he straightened up, still clutching the gash in his arm, and peeled back his lips to expose the teeth. The screaming was rooted in Leslie, too. Strong. Concentrated. Anchored.

"It's okay, Ash. Almost over."

And it was. The screeching rose, passing out of the range a human ear should be able to pick up, the sheer wrongness of it getting worse and worse.

The Second Gate was getting closer.

Reality began to tear itself apart. In a few more seconds, it would be too late.

There was only one thing he could do.

The frenetic symphony exploded, swallowing the all-too-physical *crack* of a gunshot.

THE SOUND OF rain echoed in Adrian's ears. His hair and clothes were soaked.

He'd been walking. He wasn't now.

He'd been holding something. He wasn't now.

He'd done something terrible. Nothing would ever change that.

His eyes drooped shut, then snapped open again as black hair whispered over his cheek. Whistler stared at him from approximately half an inch away, then nudged him with the flat side of one claw. *Awake?*

"Yeah," Adrian rasped. "I'm awake."

Spell-implosion. Whistler leaned back, giving their surroundings a distasteful glance.

Adrian followed suit. The basement was gone. So was the warehouse. Around them lay a fathomless darkness, pierced by two kinds of light. The First Gate was a speck in the distance, twinkling like a star. The Second…they'd been dropped almost on top of it. Shion's calculations had been impeccable until Whistler entered the equation. The woman in question was still on her feet, but barely. Redness trickled down her cheeks, melding into the black of her hair. The ritual carvings sprawled out beneath her, almost dead, the last few sparks of power leaping from the arrays. She scrubbed at her eyes and stared deep into the crack in the Gate.

"Yves?"

Adrian couldn't make himself look at the hole for too long. The pull into the darkness beyond the Gate was too strong, or maybe he was simply too weak. If he stared into it, he wouldn't be coming back. As he turned away, something squirmed through the gap. Or rather, someone. Shion's face twisted into a rictus of shock and fear. A tangle of grey skin and black steel pulled himself out with rows of skeletal arms set on an elongated body like centipede legs. Coils of black hair slithered around a cavernous face with the same plastic sheen as Whistler's. The creature that had been Yves Saunders tilted his head toward Shion and moaned like the groan of bending steel. A long, rubbery tongue flicked out to taste the air.

Familiarity? he asked.

"No, no, no, no," she repeated, stumbling back until she tripped over an ill-placed ridge. "That's not—that can't be real."

Noise, Whistler clicked. And then, directed at the other denizen from beyond death: *Desire?*

The illusion on Whistler must have gone down. Shion's head swivelled between the two of them, ignoring Adrian entirely. The new arrival slithered forward, elongated torso still partly hidden beyond the Gate, and looked at her with oil-slick eyes. She screamed and lurched backward, scrambling away from them both.

"Yves? Yves, where are you? Your face—that thing stole your face!"

The creature that had been creeping through the Gate flinched back.

Other-familiarity? he asked plaintively.

With a yell, Shion flung a burst of kinetic energy at him. It pushed him back through the hole. Or rather, Adrian thought, watching the way countless hands let go of their handholds on impact, Yves let it push him back. His black eyes flashed with hurt. Then he was gone.

The ritual was dead in full. Without charge, it was as dangerous as a child's drawing. Blood seeped slowly from Shion's eyes and ears, but she didn't appear to notice.

Disappointment. Noise. Whistler clicked again, still hovering over Adrian.

Adrian nodded and whistled softly. The screams died down as Shion lost consciousness. In the end, she hadn't been willing to accept what her other half had become. She was still breathing, at least. "What did you see?"

Enough.

"Tell me."

A sound like a boiling teakettle, compressed into a single second. *Death. Negative-self. Other-understanding.*

So that was the sound of heartbreak. Less dramatic than Adrian would have expected.

Other-understanding, Whistler repeated with a subtly different emphasis. *Correct.*

"I was right? About what?"

Self-sacrifice.

Adrian stared up at him, trying and failing to make sense of that. "I don't understand."

The response was slow, carefully constructed, very nearly a full sentence. *Leslie-death-you.*

Leslie died for you.

He understood each word individually. Strung together, their meaning escaped him. "What…what are you—?"

Disbelief? Annoyance. Proof.

For the third time, Whistler's alien senses overwrote his own. Like the second, it was a memory, but this one didn't belong to the creature from beyond the Gate. It belonged to the person Whistler had been.

❧

"Ashleigh!"

Dread. Resignation. Hope?

"Followed me, didn't you?" *Pain.* "Shouldn't have done that."

Lies. Affection. Fear.

"What is what?" *Pain.* "Don't play dumb, brat. You know this is exactly what it looks like."

Affection. Truth-stifled.

Mirror-image. Young. Fragile-but-strong. Trusting-but-wary. Observant-but-closed. Affection.

"Al's been planning this for years."

Left-street. Taken. Debt.

Desire-freedom. One-last-job.

"Ash. Bro. Idiot. It's okay."

Mirror-image. Affection. Protect.

"It's only a door. Doors are meant to be opened. All the hard work's already done. One little ritual left, and we're all good." *Lacking. Motive? Need-him-listen…* "No more killing. Unless we want to."

Anger. Shame. Pain.

Affection.

"It's okay, Ash. Almost over."

Protect. Defend. Shelter. Sacrifice. At. All. Costs.

Confusion—

Death.

❧

The sound that tore its way from Adrian's throat was more of a scream than a sob. He clawed at the nothingness around him, willing his hands to encounter resistance just so he could tear it to shreds.

His eyes burned.

"I hate you!"

No. That wasn't right. He'd simply been certain Leslie would hate him. Adrian quieted, curling into himself.

"I miss you."

That wasn't quite it, either.

"You idiot."

Better.

Proof. Whistler's hum was almost soothing despite the electric-razor whine running through it. *Apology.*

Adrian took a deep breath and released it. "Not your fault. Wasn't you."

Was. Not-current. But. Was.

"Doesn't mean I'm gonna hold you accountable for his stupid-ass decisions." And judging by what he'd learned from that packet of emotions, that really was the best term for what had been going through his brother's head. "Gods. Did he really think winning our freedom was worth that much?"

Affirmative. Whistler shuddered, a full-body twitch that brought him smoothly to a sitting position. *Debt. Shame*, he added plaintively. *Silence. Protect?*

Adrian followed suit, tugging his legs free. His jaw was clenched so tightly he could feel it in each tooth. "He should have told me. We could have left together."

Skepticism. The thought was shaky, glued together with old *fear* and *panic*, but it held. Whistler did not believe that they would have survived fleeing the Guertenas.

Adrian had to agree. He bowed his head, letting his hair fall forward. It was so damn long now. At least it could be a shield between his open wounds and the world. "We could have died together."

Together-now.

"Bit late for that. The people we were are dead in every way that matters." In a way, Adrian had killed both the Richter twins: one with a gun and one by cutting away his old life. They could never go back to being the people they once were.

Acknowledgement. A bladed claw rested gently on his hand, tip barely denting the skin. *Still. Presence.*

"I killed you."

Correction. Killed-him. Whistler coiled impossibly in on himself to peer up through Adrian's bangs. *Abandonment. Loneliness. Previous-self-incorrect.*

"What are you trying to say?"

The answer was infinitely complex and heartrendingly simple. *Stay.*

The words "I can't" were halfway out before Adrian realized what Whistler meant. "You don't want to leave?"

Affirmative.

Without thinking, Adrian's eyes flicked to the Gate above them, seeking out the gap he knew would be there. Yves had not returned, but the cracked bone was exactly where it had been earlier, still leaking its unearthly contents into the world. For all its terrible implications, he was struck by how small it was. "Don't be stupid. Your home is on the other side, isn't it? This might be your only chance to go back."

Incapable. Size. Whistler flared his wings out, ruffling the fleshy metal feathers pointedly. *Fit-negative.*

"You're scared it'll close on you again?" Adrian paused to calculate the exact dimensions of the hole and how well it synced up with the power from the shattered ritual. "I can hold it open for you. Once. It has to be now." Before too much more energy bled off, and before anyone else realized what he was doing.

Refusal. Whistler settled into Adrian's lap with an uncanny grace. The next sound he made was utterly confused, a mix of *loneliness* and *isolation* and *hopelessness.*

"What do you mean?"

Refusal, he repeated. And then, slower: *Loneliness. Isolation. Hopelessness.*

"I don't understand."

Whistler blinked, slow and catlike. He raised one bladed hand to Adrian's face and carded it through blond hair. *Show?*

Adrian hadn't realized his hair had come undone. He shoved the prickle of discomfort down and checked the Gate again. Still cracked. Still leaking. Shion lay motionless a few metres away—another pressing matter. There were a thousand other disasters that still needed fixing. So what if most of them could be delegated? He could heap it all on his shoulders until there was no room in his head for anything but his responsibilities. But that hadn't stopped Leslie from haunting Adrian before, and it wouldn't stop what he'd become from haunting Adrian now.

Instead, Adrian turned back to Whistler and nodded. "Be quick."

Once more, the world fell away. For a second time, it wasn't a single sense that was replaced—it was all of them. What they were replaced with, he couldn't say. Whistler's perceptions had been confusing enough when they were interpreting the original portal and the place between places. These memories had none of that familiarity to ground them. Beyond the Gate lay madness. Only a few scattered moments touched Adrian's conscious mind. Rotting metal. Rusting flesh. A stillness broken only by oneself. Absolute isolation. Unfathomable loneliness. A knowledge built into his structure, coursing through each delicate wire, that these things would not change. An ocean of sourceless whispers, and above them, a long, drawn-out whistle.

No wonder Whistler had linked to the Gates on contact. His whole existence had been the lowest point in his second life. That Yves had chosen that over staying showed how much Shion's rejection must have hurt.

Adrian blinked rapidly, trying to reorient himself and process that simultaneously. He only realized he was keeling over when Whistler's primary tail wrapped around his waist to prop him up.

"I have to send you back," he said, head spinning. "It's my duty as a Keeper."

Refusal. Debt. Stay.

"I owe you?" he rasped.

Whistler yawned, showing off his metallic teeth, and rested his chin on Adrian's knee. *Affirmative. Death.*

"I owe you because I killed him." That almost made sense, but…

Affirmative

"You'll be a Keeper if you stay," he cautioned. "One with the nastiest Gate token imaginable. You won't be able to walk around without an illusion. You'll have to re-learn how to communicate with people. And I—I'm not who you remember me being." That he'd finished transitioning without Leslie—that Whistler didn't even need to finish what Leslie had started—was honestly the least of the changes. "Back then, our whole lives revolved around each other, but I can't be that kind of person anymore. And I have a new partner now. You'll have to work with her, too. We'll have to get to know each other all over again."

Details, Whistler huffed. *Stay.*

Adrian closed his eyes. "All right." He let them stay shut for a few more seconds before he roused himself. "You're going to have to get off me, then."

Whistler extracted himself quickly and smoothly, sharp edges barely nicking Adrian's skin. Once free, he rose to all fours, shook himself, and paused. Again, he reached a hand that was more knife than anything else out and touched Adrian's hair. *Observation. Discomfort. Solution?*

A soft laugh died in Adrian's throat. He bowed his head. "Please."

Silver claws sliced through overgrown hair, cropping it comfortably back to ear-length.

Better?

"Yeah."

Whistler nodded and sat expectantly at the edge of the diagram. *Return?*

"Yeah," Adrian said again, hauling himself upright. "Give me a minute, and I'll send us back."

A feral grin. *Unnecessary.*

Between one moment and the next, Whistler vanished in what was unmistakably Keeper transport. Adrian stared at the empty spot. Then he began to laugh. He was still laughing as he reached down to place his hand on Shion's limp shoulder and the Gate's cold light winked out.

THE WAREHOUSE WAS almost exactly as he'd left it. The elaborate engravings had gone dead here, too, their eerie song silenced. It wouldn't be a good idea to touch them—unlike the ones etched at the foot of the Second Gate, these could still be altered and recharged. Adrian waited until he was safely off the arrays before allowing his legs to give out. He'd overstretched himself. Even with his connection to the Gates, he was about to pass out. Around him, the barrier flickered and died. He stayed right where he was, listening passively to the approaching *click* of Kade's heels.

"Matreva?"

"Not dead." Saying those two words took more out of him than he'd like to admit. "The others?"

"Not dead either. Took some doing, but I managed to tag them out. They'll be asleep for the next twenty-four hours." She peered at Matreva and let out a whistle. "You broke the ritual on her?"

"Didn't have another option." He glanced up at his partner, taking in the stress lines and the small burn on her cheekbone. "She'll live. Whistler?"

"I don't know." Kade frowned. "He vanished with you. He didn't go back through the Gate, then?"

"No, he said—"

Arrival! A new set of clicking sounds heralded Whistler's approach as he bounded toward them. He proceeded to ignore the implicit boundaries of personal space and buried his nose in Adrian's jacket. *Late.*

"—that he'd rather stay," Adrian concluded unnecessarily. *Confirmation. Together.*

Kade raised an eyebrow. "With you?"

"Where else?"

"Don't know why I'm surprised." She gave him a quick grin, then looked back at Matreva. "Her aura's shredded. Yours isn't much better."

He snorted. "Hello, pot, I'm kettle."

It wasn't an exaggeration—the faint tune of Kade's signature was off-key and faltered on every high note. She sounded at least as bad as he felt. They both needed some real sleep. Her laughter, however, was warm. "We're a mess, aren't we?"

Adrian nodded and shifted over as she sat down beside him. "Knights in shining armour, we aren't."

Whistler moved with him, still rattling contentedly. *Success.*

"True," Adrian admitted. "We did save the world."

Already, he could hear the fabric of space-time knitting back together. Taking care of Shion Matreva would be more difficult. Her coven might be released with probation due to their relative lack of dangerous knowledge, but she'd likely end up in prison for this. Given that she'd nearly destroyed the universe to bring her boyfriend back from the dead and then immediately shoved him back into the pit he'd crawled out of, Adrian didn't think she had any right to complain. He certainly wouldn't if he were in her shoes.

An uneasy quiet rolled over the remnants of the warehouse. Whistler began to hum, a meaningless noise that carried nothing but a vague sense of settling-in. The wordless melody wove in and out of the distant, muddled tune of the city. The air was cold, an unfriendly reminder that winter was approaching. Focusing on the temperature instead of his actions wouldn't help Adrian come to terms with them, he knew, but...it was late. He was tired. For the moment, his job was finished. He had the rest of his life to agonize over the things he'd done.

It was Kade who broke the silence. "The Gate's not closed, is it."

That cracked alien bone, drooling miasma, flashed through Adrian's head. "No. Not completely."

"It's not open, either."

"No."

She sighed, a drawn-out mournful sound. "We screwed up, didn't we?"

Adrian shook his head and his hair, fed up with behaving itself, attempted to strangle him. The stream of curses that followed as he wrestled it back into place earned him a faint chuckle and an amused trill. "The First Gate's been open since before recorded history," he said finally, giving up on taming the blond mess. "The Second was bound to go sooner or later."

She shot him a crooked smile. "It hasn't gone yet. The Gates aren't like dams—one crack isn't going to bring the whole thing down."

"But it will let some of—*death*—out. Just like the First Gate let whatever was behind it out way back when."

"Some of it. But not all of it. We're not looking at a full-on reality rewrite yet." Kade stretched out her arms and winced as she jarred a bruise. "Might be a good thing. Whistler's still here, after all. Having a trickle of whatever that stuff is might make things easier for him."

Possible, Whistler tossed in. *Unlikely.*

Adrian tilted his head, searching out a gleam of silver. "Is that going to be a problem? Not having enough of it?"

Bone-white shoulders rolled in a shrug. *Uncertainty. Enthusiasm!*

Despite everything, Adrian found himself grinning. When he looked up, Kade was watching them, an odd smile on her lips. "You two are looking awful cozy."

"You were the one who wanted a third Keeper for this area."

"I was, wasn't I? There gonna be room for me still? I can tell there's a ton of baggage between you."

Affirmative, Whistler chirped. Then he sat back and took one of Kade's hands.

She flinched, but let him. "Three's a powerful number, but it's also an unbalanced one, and we need all the stability we can get."

"Four's a powerful number, too. Symbolizes death."

Whistler gave him a flat stare. *Improvement-required.*

Kade snickered. "Don't be too hard on him. I'm the quippy one in this partnership, Whistler."

Grave-responsibility. Respect.

"I know," she agreed. "It's a great and terrible burden, but some-body has to do it." When she turned her eyes back to Adrian, she didn't move her hands away. "The Second Gate's cracked and we were at ground zero. It's not like we can turn down extra help."

"No matter where it comes from?" Adrian prodded.

"I know I've been a little weird about him. I'll get over it. Can't be mean to my new partner, can I?"

Affirmative, Whistler threw in. *Partners.*

"We'll be fine. And just think—by this time tomorrow, there'll be a brand-new crisis for us to run ourselves ragged over. Lucky us!"

Adrian let out a heartfelt groan and slumped forward, resting his chin on the top of Whistler's head. Leslie would have dumped him on his ass and laughed; Whistler squeaked, then pressed back with a low, metallic purr. Not the same. But not bad, either. "The problem with saving the world is that it doesn't stay saved."

Boring-negative, Whistler contributed. *Purpose. Excitement!*

Adrian smiled. "You're going to eat those words."

About the Author:
Nicola Kapron

Nicola Kapron has previously been published by *Neo-opsis Science Fiction Magazine*, *Rebel Mountain Press*, *Soteira Press*, *All Worlds Wayfarer*, *Mannison Press*, and more. Nicola lives in British Columbia with a hoard of books—mostly fantasy and horror—and an extremely fluffy cat.

Links

Personal Website: https://www.nicolakapronportfolio.com/

Titles by Nicola Kapron:

The Act of Salvation
Be Not Afraid
Campfire Stories
Dead Man's Bells
The Deadman's Gambit
In Good Company
It's Witchcraft! (forthcoming)
The Little Wolf and Red (forthcoming)
More Than We Deserve
The Ocean Went on Forever
RE: Sleeping Beauty
Scrap Metal Angel
User Error

Anthologies Including Nicola Kapron:

Aether Beyond the Binary (author contributor)

About Duck Prints Press LLC

Duck Prints Press LLC is an independent publisher based in New York State. Our founding vision is to help fanwork creators navigate the complex process of bringing their original works from first draft to print, culminating in publishing their work under our imprint. We are particularly dedicated to working with queer creators and publishing stories and artwork featuring characters from across the LGBTQIA+ spectrum.

Support Duck Prints Press on Patreon!

Find us online at our website https://duckprintspress.com/ or on social media:

Bluesky: duckprintspress.bsky.social
Facebook: duckprintspress
Instagram: duckprintspress
Patreon: duckprintspress
TikTok: @duckprintspress
Tumblr: duckprintspress

Goodreads: https://www.goodreads.com/user/show/129902473-duck-prints-press-llc
Storygraph: https://app.thestorygraph.com/profile/unforth

If you enjoyed this story, don't forget to leave us a review!